Tangled Disasters
Sapphire City Series Book Three
L.R. Crow

Phoenix Voices Publishing

Copyright © 2024 by L.R. Crow

All rights reserved.

No part of this publication may be reproduced, distributed, or transmitted in any form or by any means, including photocopying, recording, or other electronic or mechanical methods, without the prior written permission of the publisher, except as permitted by U.S. copyright law. For permission requests, contact Phoenix Voices Publishing, 7901 4th St. N, St. Petersburg, FL, 33702, 727-222-0090.

The story, all names, characters, and incidents portrayed in this production are fictitious. No identification with actual persons (living or deceased), places, buildings, and products is intended or should be inferred.

L.R. Crow asserts the moral right to be identified as the author of this work.

L.R. Crow has no responsibility for the persistence or accuracy of URLs for external or third-party Internet Websites referred to in this publication and does not guarantee that any content on such Websites is, or will remain, accurate or appropriate.

Designations used by companies to distinguish their products are often claimed as trademarks. All brand names and product names used in this book and on its cover are trade names, service marks, trademarks, and registered trademarks of their respective owners. The publishers and the book are not associated with any product or vendor mentioned in this book. None of the companies referenced within the book have endorsed the book.

Contents

1. Trigger Warnings   3
2. Chapter One   4
3. Chapter Two   14
4. Chapter Three   23
5. Chapter Four   30
6. Chapter Five   41
7. Chapter Six   49
8. Chapter Seven   58
9. Chapter Eight   69
10. Chapter Nine   78
11. Chapter Ten   86
12. Chapter Eleven   95
13. Chapter Thirteen   104
14. Chapter Fourteen   113
15. Chapter Fifteen   123

16. Chapter Sixteen 132
17. Chapter Seventeen 141
18. Chapter Eighteen 151
19. Chapter Nineteen 160
20. Chapter Twenty 170
21. Also by L.R. Crow 178

Trigger Warnings

This novel has elements that may be triggering to some. Themes throughout this novel include sex, scenes of graphic BDSM, adult language, suicide, alcohol, and abuse. If any of these topics are triggering to you, proceed with caution.

Chapter One

A Struggling Family

A LONG TIME AGO, in a far-off land, lived an impoverished couple. They lived a simple life, but often, they were left wanting for more. Food was scarce in their neck of the woods; somehow, they always made it work, until now. They stared across the clearing at an old witch's cottage. Across the way was a bountiful garden on her land with fruit trees, vegetables, grains, and the works.

"She wouldn't notice if we only took a few things, would she," he whispered to his wife.

"She's a witch; do you *really* want to risk it," she cautioned him.

"For you, I would do anything," he embraced her, kissing her head.

"I am famished," his wife admitted.

They had not eaten in three days. The couple was struggling to make ends meet. They always wanted a child to call their own, but they could not fathom bringing a child onto this earth in their current situation.

Neither of them had the strength to make it into Sapphire City, just a few miles away. They had been sick for some time, although their throaty coughs seemed to be finally clearing up.

"Adam, those peaches do look divine," Eve said, ogling at the fruit trees.

"That's it; I can't take it anymore," Adam sighed.

Eve watched as he walked out the door into the warm spring sun. The way the light illuminated his skin always took her breath away. She remembered when they were married, looking him in the eyes as the sun's rays touched them. The way he looked at her still hangs in her mind. He looks at her that way every day, but her wedding day was the most memorable.

He promised to always take care of her, no matter what. This is what he was trying to do. She watched Adam creep across the pasture toward the witch's cottage. Stopping only to cough in his sleeve.

Adam climbed the fence into the witch's lavish garden. Soon, he disappeared into the greenery and the lines of fruit trees. Eve was nervous that something might happen to him, and she watched in anticipation. She hoped he would make it back un-hexed.

Just when she began to lose hope, she watched her husband emerge from the garden holding armfuls of fruit and a few vegetables. He even grabbed wheat to mill into flour. Adam always loved his wife's homemade bread.

Adam jogged for the house, waving for his wife to meet him at the door. His wife swung the door open so he could step into the safety of their home. Eve grabbed as many fruits as she could, helping her husband to avoid bruising the fruit by dropping it on the ground.

She placed them into an old fruit bowl she had received from her grandmother for a wedding gift. Nostalgia tugged at her heartstrings as she remembered Sundays with her grandmother. She would sit in her lap for story time, always listening close to the fairytales her grandmother spun for her. They would then nap together on the floor in the living room.

This was Eve's favorite day of the week.

Oh, how she missed her grandmother now.

"Eve," Adam called, snapping her out of her reverie. "What do you want me to make for dinner tonight?"

"I always did love your green bean medley," she swooned.

"For you, my love, I would set fire to the world," he whisked away, singing.

Adam went straight to work chopping vegetables and throwing them into a pan. Eve could smell the herbs and spices filling the air of their home. The smell had both of their mouths watering and their stomachs growling.

Eve went to work, preparing and milling the wheat. It took her some time to grind it down into the fine powder for bread. It always amazed her what her hands could do with wheat and other grains. By the time she was finished pouring the flour into its container, her husband was setting food on the table. "Eve," he sang to her. "Tonight, we dine like royalty."

"I love the sound of that," Eve stood up, headed for the table.

Eve always loved when her husband was happy. His smile took every worry from her mind and filled her heart with unconditional love. The married couple sat and supped together, enjoying the flavor of the food and the warmth of each other's company. Eve grabbed the dishes and silverware as they finished eating and headed to the sink. She washed the plates, Adam dried them, and they put them away together.

When Eve stepped into the living room, Adam hugged her from behind, his erection pressing into her backside. The happiness he felt from being able to feed his small family was evident.

"I want all of you tonight," he whispered to her.

Eve felt a shiver run up her spine as he said this. Tingles were starting to take over her bits. She found it unfair how he could make her melt with a few short words. She was trapped under his spell, and nothing made her happier.

She pushed herself back into him, enjoying the sensation of his erection against her backside.

"Mmm," she said. "I love the hold you have on me."

Adam spun his beautiful red-haired wife around and kissed her deeply. His hands gravitated toward her breasts to find her nipples fully erect. He loved the delicious feeling of her body responding to his touch.

Adam took his wife's hand and led her to the bedroom. Once there, he tugged his shirt over his head and removed hers. The lustful look in her eyes made his dick throb even more. The two quickly undressed and lay in the bed.

Adam held her in his arms for a few minutes before he turned her face with his hand.

"Kiss me," he said to her.

Eve pressed her lips into his, forcing his mouth open with her dainty tongue. Adam returned the kiss, groaning into her mouth. Adam sat up on the bed as Eve climbed on top of him. She pushed her bits onto his throbbing erection. She grabbed his hair and tugged at it as he thrust deeper into her.

When she threw her head back in pleasure, he sucked on her nipples. He reached down and used his thumb to gently circle her clit. After an hour of moans and screams, the two of them climaxed in unison. Eve's juices poured down her thighs and all over her husband.

"You are the most beautiful woman I know," Adam told her as he kissed her gently.

Eve climbed off her husband and headed for the shower, where Adam joined her. He turned her back toward the water and tilted her head back as he washed her hair. He continued washing her body, ensuring she was clean before he cleaned himself. Once they were both clean, he grabbed a towel, dried his wife off, then dried himself.

They climbed into bed with full stomachs and clean bodies and drifted off to sleep. Adam tossed and turned that night; he dreamt of going hungry and being unable to care for his wife.

He woke up a few times to watch her sleep.

Eve awoke first the following day. She headed to the kitchen to prepare breakfast. Adam had even found eggs in the coop near the witch's garden. Eve began cooking eggs and cutting up fruit for breakfast. Adam woke up to the smell of breakfast and left the bedroom to sit at the table.

"Good morning, my love," he told Eve.

"Hello, babe," she replied.

She served her husband with a plate of eggs and fruit. When done, she hiked back to the kitchen and made her plate. All Eve wanted was fruit. She grabbed peaches, oranges, and apples from the bowl of fruit she had sliced. She continued to make herself a fruit salad to eat for breakfast. They ate breakfast together in peace.

"I have to go out and find work today," Adam mentioned.

"I wish we never had to work," Eve said hopefully.

"Wouldn't that be a dream," Adam chuckled.

Adam rose from the table and kissed his wife goodbye. On his way out of the house, he placed his dish and utensils in the sink. Once the door shut, he walked down a path to Sapphire City. He had not been to town in weeks due to being sick for so long.

Winter had snuck up on him, and the cold winter air took his breath away. He looked at the lines of tall buildings, wondering which he should start his job search. He saw a woman with raven-black hair and rosy cheeks as he wandered. She was with a little man, and they were headed into a pub.

He continued past the pub and walked into a department store. The store was decorated with garland and lights to bring the holiday cheer. Adam approached the counter.

"I'd like to apply for a job, please," he said to the blonde behind the counter.

The girl took one look at his disheveled appearance and rolled her eyes. Adam was confused by her lack of compassion.

"We aren't hiring," she told him with an attitude.

"Thank you, anyway," Adam tipped his hat to her and walked away.

He knew a job would not be easy to find, but he was still disappointed she would not let him apply. He opened the large glass doors to the department store, wondering where to try next.

His mind wandered back to the woman and the small man he saw. Next, he thought to gain employment at the pub across town. He walked a few blocks in the other direction and peeked into the pub window. When he stepped from the window, the wind blew his hat away before he could catch it. He chased after it but had no luck in getting it back. When he returned to the pub, he pushed the oak door open and was assaulted with the smell of greasy food. His stomach growled in response.

Adam walked up to the bar and flagged down the bartender.

He found himself nervous as he did so.

"How can I help you," the bartender asked as he looked him up and down.

Adam's disheveled appearance took the man behind the counter by surprise. He knew instantly that his life was difficult.

"I'd like to apply for a job, please," Adam replied.

The bartender looked at the other end of the room. He did not want to disappoint Adam but could tell he was not fit to work in a pub.

"The owner isn't here today," he lied. "You can try back next week when he returns from vacation." "Thank you," Adam responded.

Adam left the pub disgruntled. He could not care for his wife if he could not find a job. This left him with feelings of incompetence.

Three Months Later

Despite not finding a job, Adam's time with his wife had been beautiful. Spring was approaching, and the weather was warming up. The first of the flowers had started to sprout from the ground. The two were struggling to keep afloat. Both were thankful that they owned the cottage outright.

"Should I sneak back into the witch's garden," he asked his wife.

"I have been extra hungry lately," Eve admitted. "I am late." "You're what," Adam asked, unsure whether to smile or cry.

"Haven't you noticed," she asked, rubbing her stomach.

Adam hadn't noticed that her stomach had grown; he had always been focused on her beauty. He felt a sense of pride finding out that his wife was pregnant, but they were already stealing food as it was. Adam sighed.

"I'm headed to the garden. Wish me luck," he forced a laugh.

"Be careful, please," Eve cautioned him.

Eve waited in quiet anticipation as Adam went to the witch's garden. She hoped he would find more eggs this time, they had been her biggest craving over the past few months. Her mouth was watering, thinking of the delicious peaches on the trees on the witch's land.

After what seemed like hours, Adam emerged from the garden with a large basket full of food. He was wise enough to bring a basket to carry everything. He knew they would need plenty if it would last through the week.

"I felt like you needed a good source of protein to support our growing child," Adam smiled warmly at his wife.

"It's like you read my mind; I have been craving eggs every day for the past few months," Eve said gratefully.

Adam reached his arms out for Eve and pulled her into him. He kissed her on the forehead and looked into her bright green eyes. The sparkle in them never faded, even though they were struggling.

"I love you, Eve," he whispered to her.

"I love you, too, Adam," she gently kissed his lips as she said this.

The couple continued unpacking the basket of food Adam had foraged from the witch's garden. Adam placed the eggs in a bowl on the counter while Eve put the fruit away. She sauntered over to the bowl of eggs and picked up the bowl, smiling.

"Would you like some eggs," she asked her husband.

"I would love nothing more," he replied.

Eve cooked an omelet with vegetables and cut up some fruit for each of them. Adam and Eve enjoyed each other's company as they ate their breakfast. When Adam finished his omelet and fruit, he kissed his wife and donned his coat and gloves.

"Where are you going," Eve asked concernedly.

"I had no luck on the job front the other day, and I MUST find something if we are going to survive," he said. "The witch will start noticing that her food is missing from her garden, and who knows what she will do when she figures it out."

"You are right, Adam. Please be careful in town," she embraced her husband before he left.

Adam opened the door and slid outside. The fresh spring air gave him the confidence he needed to search for a source of income in town.

Chapter Two

The Price of Theft

Adam secured a job at a rundown factory deep in the heart of Sapphire City. The work was difficult, and the hours were long; he was often exhausted by the time he arrived home. Although he knew this was what they needed to survive. After work each day, he picked up food from the local market and headed home to his wife. He was always filled with dust and grime from working in the poorest part of the factory, yet he was proud to have a job to call his own.

His wife was growing by the day, and he loved to rub her stomach in the evenings when he arrived home from work. Eve had been sick for most of the pregnancy, and she would go into labor any day now. Adam put in for a few days off and was granted his wishes.

Adam was startled awake when he heard his wife screech in pain.

"Call the midwife," she told him. "The baby is coming."

Adam rushed off to the rotary phone in the living room and dialed the midwife as quickly as he could.

"Hello," he heard on the other end of the phone.

"Hello, Griselda," he greeted her. "The baby is coming. Can you make it here in time?"

"I will be there as quickly as I can," she hung up the phone before Adam could mutter another word.

Adam prepared the bedroom for the arrival of the baby. He placed many blankets on the bed to prevent the mattress from becoming bloody after the baby arrived. He grabbed warm, clean rags and a comfortable gown for Eve to change into. He helped her to change into the hospital gown; she was in too much pain to get out of bed.

The midwife arrived quicker than either of them thought she would. She must have ridden in by horse. Her cheeks were flushed from riding in the wind. Her hair was ruffled, but she was ready to help deliver the baby. She brought a stethoscope, supplies to clean Eve and the baby, and a pair of umbilical scissors to cut the baby's cord.

"Welcome, Griselda," Eve said between painful contractions.

"Hello, Eve," she replied. "Are we ready to get this baby out," she asked.

Both new parents nodded as she said this. It had been a rough nine months, but Adam was grateful for everything he had, especially his job. This gave him the means to support his family, and that was all he wanted.

Eve spent hours in labor; the midwife stayed at her side every step of the way. After four hours of intense contractions, Eve was ready to push. Adam hated seeing his wife in so much pain but felt nothing but pure unconditional love as he watched the baby's head crown. He saw a beautiful head of silky blonde hair as Eve continued to push. Adam stopped holding his breath when he heard the baby take its first few breaths and begin to cry.

When the baby was on Eve's chest, the midwife motioned for Adam to come close. She clamped the umbilical cord and handed Adam the scissors.

"Did you want to cut the cord," she asked him.

"I would love to," Adam stepped forward.

He felt an immense amount of pride as he cut his child's umbilical cord. The midwife soon whisked her away to be weighed and cleaned up. When she returned, the baby was swaddled in a pink blanket. Adam noticed her bright blonde hair and sapphire blue eyes.

"Congratulations, Daddy," the midwife turned toward him with the baby. "It's a girl."

Adam heard his wife crying tears of joy in the background. He couldn't help but cry as well. He was proud of his wife and happy to be a father. Since the two of them had met, all he had wanted was to create a happy family together. He felt they were on the path to a blessed and wonderful life.

"She is beautiful," Adam stated. "Just like her mother."

He walked over to his wife and planted a kiss on her lips. He was filled with love and pride as he watched his newborn baby girl suckle on her mother's breast. There was no greater feeling than becoming a father. He pulled a chair close to his wife and ran his fingers through her beautiful copper hair.

"I am so proud of you," he said to her. "I am so proud to have you as my wife," he cooed at her.

Adam kissed his wife on the cheek and touched the baby's head as she ate.

"We have to think of a name," he said. "But it can wait until you are more rested."

"I am exhausted," Eve admitted.

After the baby finished feeding, she handed her to Adam. He found himself nervous to hold a fragile life in his hands. He held her close and sang to her as he sat on the bed beside his wife.

"I feel like my life is now complete," he said as he looked at Eve in pure adoration.

He watched her sigh in contentment as she drifted off to sleep. When he knew she was resting well, he rose from the bed and took the baby into the next room. He headed to the couch and snuggled with his newborn daughter. He envisioned all the fun times they would have as his child grew up. He found himself wondering what she would be like as an adult. He shook these thoughts from his head. He wanted to enjoy her in the moment and not create the anxiety of thinking ahead.

When Eve awoke, her breasts ached. It was time for the baby to eat once again. She beckoned her husband into their bedroom, and he handed her their daughter. Adam's face fell when he realized how much they needed for their child.

"I will be back, my love," he said. "Our baby needs a bed and some new clothes."

"Okay, Adam," Eve said. "Be careful; I will see you when you get home."

Adam exited the house and went down the familiar path to Sapphire City. He didn't know how he would afford it, but he had to bring home a bed for his new baby girl. A light dinged above his head as he thought of cutting lumber to build the baby a crib. Surely, this would be cheaper than the astronomical prices the department store would charge.

He knew he would have time to build the baby a bed as Eve would spend hours holding the baby and bonding with her. Adam wandered in the woods beside Sapphire City. He chopped enough wood and bundled it together with cords to carry them home.

When Adam arrived home, he was sweaty and dirty. It was much work chopping wood to build a crib. He walked to his small shack beside his home and grabbed tools to sand and one to shape the bed into the design he envisioned in his mind. He always was good with his hands.

After hours of cutting, sanding, and shaping, he had created a cradle that the child would fit in until she was at least three years old. When he carried the cradle into the house, he brought it into their bedroom. He grabbed the small mattress Eve had crafted while she was pregnant and placed it in the cradle.

Eve ogled at the baby's bed, noticing the moons and stars Adam had crafted into the headboard. She couldn't believe the craftsmanship of the bed; it was better than any bed he could have purchased at the department store.

"This bed is beautiful, Adam," Eve told him as he set the cradle beside them.

"Only the best for my darling baby girl," Adam said as he looked at his baby.

It was close to nightfall when he finished setting everything up. He put away the clothes he had found in town earlier and headed to the shower. While in the bathroom, he called out to his wife.

"Do you need anything before I clean up, my love," he asked his wife.

"I think I am okay," she shouted back to her husband as she covered the baby's ears.

Eve snuggled close to the baby as she lay in bed. She looked into her beautiful blue eyes and soaked up the appearance of her entire feet. When the baby awoke, she laid her on the bed. She took the blanket off her and looked at her little feet and toes.

"I have never seen anything so beautiful in my life," she said aloud. "You need a name, but I feel no name is perfect enough for my little girl."

Eve picked her child up and brushed her nose against her child's nose. She saw a small smile when she pulled the baby away from her face. This warmed her heart to see her baby smiling back at her. As she placed her back down on the bed, she watched her yawn, and her tiny mouth opened wide, revealing her tongue inside.

"So precious," Eve heard from beside her.

When she looked over, she saw Adam staring down at their daughter. A smile crossed her face as she watched Adam interact with the baby. Later that evening, Eve fed the baby before she settled down to rest. The couple knew they would be up often at night for the first few years of their child's life.

They heard loud thumps at the door as they drifted off to sleep. Adam rose from bed to see who could be at the door at this ungodly hour of the night. When he opened the door, he saw a middle-aged woman with dark, wiry hair and wild green eyes. She wore a dark cloak, and Adam felt unsafe in her presence. He thought she looked familiar, but he could not place where he had known her from.

"Hello, Adam," she said forcefully.

"Hi," Adam said nervously.

"I have seen you stealing food from my garden," she stated.

"Don't you know that stealing is wrong?"

Adam wanted to slam the door in her face, board the windows, and block the entrance. But something kept him standing there staring at the witch. He feared what she might do to them since she had figured out that they were taking food from her garden.

"Please don't hurt my wife," he said nervously.

"Oh, I don't intend to lay a hand or a hex on anyone," the witch said calmly. "But there is a price to pay for theft." Adam stepped back in fear.

"Wha—, what could that price possibly be," he asked the witch.

The two of them listened as the baby woke up. Adam watched the witch's expression glow. The witch tapped her chin for a moment before she spoke up.

"The price for your thievery is...," the witch started. "Your firstborn child, give her to me."

Adam nearly fainted hearing these words. He could not believe another human could be so cruel. He would give anything else to the witch, but not his child.

"Absolutely not," Adam said sternly.

"That's what you think," the witch backed away laughing.

Adam slammed and locked the door and ensured the windows were also locked. No witch would be entering their home or taking their baby. He walked to the bedroom and snuggled close to his wife and child, fearful of what might come next.

Eve awoke with a bone-chilling feeling that something was wrong. When she glanced toward the window, she saw a middle-aged woman watching her family sleep. She rubbed her eyes to be sure she was not imagining things. When she opened her eyes back up, the woman was gone. Eve figured she was still half asleep and laid back down to rest.

The baby started crying an hour later, ready to be fed. Eve grabbed a diaper and changed the baby before she left the room to feed her daughter on the couch. Adam needed sleep; he had to return to work the next day.

Eve fell asleep feeding the baby on the couch. Morning time crept up quicker than she expected. Adam kissed her on the head on his way out to work. He looked back at his small family, wishing he could spend another day home with them. But that was not going to pay the bills.

"Be safe, Adam," Eve called after him.

"I love you, Eve," he called back to her. "I will see my two beautiful ladies when I arrive home this evening. I miss you already."

"Bye, Adam, we love you too," she replied.

Eve watched as her husband slowly closed the door. When he was gone, she looked down at her sleeping child and smiled. She leaned down and kissed her on the forehead. She stood from the couch, taking care not to wake the baby as she moved. When she entered the bedroom, she placed the baby in the cradle to nap.

As the baby was napping, Eve prepared breakfast. She had to keep healthy if she was going to breastfeed her child. She prepared eggs and toast and grabbed a juicy peach from the bowl on the table. As she finished her last bite, she heard the heartwarming sound of her child's hungry cries.

Eve placed her dishes in the sink and made her way to her bedroom, where the baby was lying in the cradle. She lifted her daughter out of the cradle and lay in bed with her to feed her. She smiled as she heard the baby's coos and noises of contentment as she fed.

Soon enough, Eve and the baby were both asleep. They were in a peaceful dreamland, and the rest was well-needed by both after a long night of ups and downs.

Chapter Three

A Hard Lesson Learned

Eve slept hard after feeding her child. She was in such a deep sleep that nothing besides her child's cry could wake her. The baby lay beside her in a peaceful slumber. The two of them were blissful in their sleep. Unaware of the witch watching them through the window. The witch had her eye on the prize, and she would get her hands on that child if it were the last thing she did.

Adam had never mentioned who was at the door that evening, so Eve left the door unlocked. They had never had trouble with theft or intruders before, and she felt safe in their quaint home. As she and the child slept, the witch quietly entered the house. Her heart raced as she got closer to Eve's room. She was so light on her foot that a mouse sounded like an elephant walking in comparison to her.

She stood at the foot of the bed, watching the baby sleep next to her mother. She noticed that there was space between the two of them, making it easier for her to scoop up the baby and head out of the house. Eve stirred in her sleep, worrying the witch that she might wake up. She waited for Eve to settle before she walked to the side of the bed and picked up the baby. She had always wanted a child of her own, but she couldn't conceive.

Lucky for her, the young girl was a heavy sleeper. The witch made her way out of the room carefully and headed for the door. As she got to the door, it opened. She stood face to face with Adam, whose mouth fell open.

"Give me my child," he roared at the witch.

Adam reached for the baby. He was livid to see the witch standing in his house holding his baby girl. The witch pulled the baby out of his grasp.

"I will not; she is my child now," she screeched.

Adam thought of attacking the witch, but he did not want to hurt his sleeping child in her arms. He watched the witch cuddle his daughter and coo at her.

"The price of your thievery is your first-born child," she hissed.

Adam looked at the ground in defeat. He knew his efforts would be quashed in his attempt to get the baby back. The witch pushed him out of the way as she scurried out of the house, laughing. Adam watched her escape into the night, wishing he could have changed things somehow.

Adam fell to the ground. He felt he had lost everything when the witch walked away with his baby. Adam sobbed for hours before his wife awoke. He heard her panicking in the bedroom, but he could not pick himself up off the floor to console her.

"ADAM, where is the baby," she asked in a fluster.

Adam couldn't respond; he was too embarrassed and heartbroken to admit that the witch kidnapped their child right in front of him. There was no way he could have fought back without hurting the baby. Once again, Adam failed his family.

As Eve emerged from the bedroom, she saw her husband on the floor in tears. She ran to his side and sat with him, worried about the words that were about to escape his lips.

"You were sleeping so peacefully last night that I didn't tell you the witch came to the door," he sobbed.

"What," she said, shocked.

"She knows that we had been stealing food from her," he admitted. "She said the price for our crimes was our first born child. I told her no and slammed the door and locked the door and windows last night. All these days of eating food and enjoying our lives, she has been watching us. She has been waiting for the perfect moment to swoop in and destroy everything that we have together, and it is my own fault."

Tears started welling in Eve's eyes. Her heart shattered into a million pieces; there was no coming back from losing her child to the poor choices they made to survive the winter. She had never thought another human would destroy their lives by stealing their baby.

"Please never feel like any of this is your fault. We were only doing what we needed to do to survive, and I love you for that," she told him.

She wiped a tear from her eye, but they kept falling. All she could think about was the pride she felt when she brought her baby into the world. There is no better feeling than that of being a mother. She knew Adam had felt the same way about being a father. This moment brought them closer together than they had ever been. But her heart and soul were consumed by darkness and grief.

"I cannot fathom a life without our sweet little girl," Eve cried.

Eve shook and sobbed in her husband's arms. The two of them were broken souls and did not know how they would ever come back from this. All the pain of their child being gone was too much.

"Please don't speak like that," Adam caressed her face and looked into her eyes.

All the while, he had the same thoughts rolling through his mind. He wanted anything but to live after losing their precious gift from the gods.

The mourning couple climbed into bed in the wee hours of the morning and fell asleep in each other's arms. That night, they dreamed of darkness and misery. The witch taking their child played repeatedly in Adam's mind. He felt he should have done something differently, but what could he have done?

The sun peeked through the window earlier than expected the following day. Neither of them wanted to get out of bed; they were too distraught to move. But Adam had to work. He did not know how he was going to focus on working when all he could think about was losing his child. He also worried about Eve, he was terrified of something happening to her, too.

Adam kissed his wife on the forehead before preparing for work. He threw on his clothes and rushed out the door in fear of being late for work. As he arrived in Sapphire City, he saw a disgruntled-looking queen walking out of an off-beat bed and breakfast down the block from his work. He couldn't help but wonder what made her so upset. Most of him didn't care because his child was stolen from him. But part of his mind cared about people in general and reminded him that life is precious and important.

He couldn't wait to get home to Eve that evening. He needed to feel the warmth of his embrace to make it through the night. His day had felt longer than usual, and he kept messing everything up at work. Being an efficient worker was not in the cards for today, and he was glad to be out of there. His boss was not happy with him but understood the circumstances and let him slide. He arrived at the house shortly after dusk.

When he stepped closer to their home, he realized the door was ajar. He found this odd after the happenings of the previous night. He entered his home worried for his wife's safety and well-being. Panic filled his entire body. He didn't see her in the kitchen or on the couch.

What he dreaded most was what he found when he entered the bedroom. When he walked in, he saw a sheet hanging from the ceiling. The sheet was wrapped around his wife's neck, and she was cold and blue. There was nothing he could do to bring her back to life.

Adam screamed bloody murder as he watched his wife hang from the ceiling. When he was able to move from his spot, he grabbed a ladder and cut his wife down from the ceiling. He laid her in the bed and hugged her cold body for hours as he sobbed. Now, he had nothing and no one in the world.

Adam fell asleep as he held his wife's lifeless body. Instead of being a place of comfort and love, their bed was now a cold, empty space with pieces of his broken heart scattered all around. When he slept that night, he dreamt of the witch. He saw the smug look on her face as she told him the repercussions of his thievery. He tossed and turned all night long. When he awoke the following morning, the reality of her death hit him all over again. Adam spent the day rocking back and forth, holding his knees, and crying. He carefully wrapped his wife in the sheet and dragged her outside. He spent hours digging a deep enough hole to bury his wife in. He crafted a headstone for her as well.

He headed for the cottage door. When he was inside his home, intense feelings of sadness and dread filled his soul. He missed his little girl more than anything. The day she was brought into this world was the proudest moment in his young life.

His beautiful wife was now six feet under the ground. She was cold and stiff, whereas he was warm with a beating heart. Losing Eve and the baby meant losing all of himself. He felt lost and alone. Adam felt his chances at happiness in his life were gone. He didn't want to sleep, he couldn't eat, he couldn't even bring himself to shower.

He could still see the witch in his doorway, laughing and holding his baby girl. Adam could still see her scurrying away in the night. The baby never awoke; she slept so peacefully through the events of the evening. He had never felt so defeated in his life.

"I just don't want to live anymore," he said aloud to himself.

These thoughts scared the life out of him. He had never been suicidal in his life. But, he had never lost everything in a matter of days, either.

Dark circles could be seen under his eyes. Each time he closed them, he saw his wife and child. Every second of every day would feel like an eternity without them.

He was a zombie by this point, and grief and anger had consumed his heart and soul. He walked over to the cabinet where he kept his hunting guns. He went into the kitchen, stood up the gun, and put his mouth over it. He shook as he stood there; he was terrified. But he'd be damned if he lived in the cottage by himself without a family to call his own.

His hand slipped. His entire life flashed before his eyes as the trigger went off. Blood sprayed all over the kitchen, and remnants of his skull and brain hit the floor. Adam and Eve were no more. They couldn't bear a life without their child, and now they didn't have to.

Their baby would live a life not knowing her parents. She would never know how much they loved her. She would never know the truth; she was left to live her life with an evil, selfish witch.

Chapter Four

"Mother Gothel"

M ADAM GOTHEL RAN DEEP into the night. She knew she wouldn't be returning to the home she had stayed in her entire life. She did not want Adam and Eve to find their child and try to take her back. She now had a baby girl to call her own. Although, she had no idea what this meant for her or the child or how it would all pan out.

The wiry, dark-haired witch stopped in her place to look down at the precious bundle of joy in her arms. She instantly fell in love when a large pair of sapphire eyes stared back at her. She found it odd how much hair such a young baby had. It was bright blonde, and it glimmered in the moonlight. The hair flowed down to just below her cheekbones. Normally, a baby her age with blonde hair looked nearly bald.

Deep within the forest on the outskirts of Sapphire City, she found a small, abandoned castle. She made this small place into a home for her baby. It was a difficult night; the baby was up and down. She was hungry, and Madam Gothel had hardly any milk to give her. She knew in the morning they would have to travel into Sapphire City and shop for everything a child would need.

It was early when they started their day. The sun peeked through the window in the tower as they opened their eyes. Madam Gothel had never felt so complete in all her lonely years. She looked down at her child and smiled.

"Rapunzel," she cooed. "That is the perfect name for a beautiful child like you."

The soft coos of the baby in her arms filled her heart with glee.

"It is time for us to travel into town and gather the items you need," Gothel spoke softly to her child.

Lucky for Rapunzel, Gothel was a mastermind at auctioning rare items and sometimes people. She had plenty of money to support their life together. Gothel went all out at a store called Once Upon a Fairytale. The place was full to the brim with all the baby furniture and items a child would need until they were at least ten years old.

Madam Gothel pointed at the perfect crib for her child. She told them where to deliver it to and set a time for later that evening when she would be home. Gothel filled a cart with diapers, supplies, and an array of stunning princess clothes for her little girl.

When they finished at that store, it was time they headed to the grocer for formula and food to fill the fridge to sustain herself while she raised Rapunzel. After the shopping was complete, Rapunzel and Mother Gothel headed home.

She just barely got the door open when Rapunzel started to cry.

"Alright, sweetie," she said to Rapunzel. "Mamas got your milk right here."

Gothel placed Rapunzel on a blanket on the floor. She opened the bottles that she had just purchased and washed them in the sink. She poured formula into a bottle, lifted a crying Rapunzel from her spot and began to feed her.

The sweet noises coming from Rapunzel melted Mother Gothel's heart. Remembering to burp the child, she took the bottle from Rapunzel's mouth and sat her up, patting her back. She heard a few small burps come from Rapunzel as she wiggled and whined for her bottle back.

When Rapunzel finished eating, Gothel heard a tap at the door. With Rapunzel in her arms, she opened the door, and the men had arrived with the crib. She was glad to see them, as her arms were growing tired, and she hated placing her sweet baby girl on the blanket on the floor.

They assembled the crib, carried the walking chair into the room, and set it near the crib.

"Thank you so much," Gothel said gratefully.

"It is our pleasure, ma'am," a light-haired young man replied.

The men turned and left, closing the door behind him. Gothel held Rapunzel close, walking over to the rocking chair. She rocked with the baby, singing quietly to her until she fell asleep. When Rapunzel was asleep, she placed her in the crib for a nap.

When the baby was napping, Gothel laid down, too. It had been an exhausting day. She had only just begun to drift off when she heard Rapunzel squirming. Thankfully, Rapunzel drifted back off to sleep so the new mother could sleep as well.

Five Years Later

Rapunzel was growing into a beautiful young girl. Her golden blonde hair had grown to just below her bottom. Mother Gothel attempted to trim her hair to keep it healthy and was taken aback when the shears would not cut through it. Gothel looked at her daughter in shock.

"What's wrong, Mama," Rapunzel looked up at her mother's confused face.

"It's your hair," she gasped. "I knew there was something special about you."

"You always tell me I'm special, Mama," Rapunzel smiled at her mother.

"You are, my dear, you are my very special and precious little girl," Gothel cooed at her daughter.

Mother Gothel grabbed the brush and began to brush Rapunzel's beautiful hair. She pondered how powerful her child's hair might be. It was nearly nightfall, and the young girl was getting ready for bed. Rapunzel brushed her teeth and ran back into the main room with her mother.

When she reached the center of the room, the moonlight shone upon her hair. Gothel remembered when she was running with her as a baby. The moon made her hair glimmer.

"Magical," she said, deep in thought.

"Magical, Mama. What do you mean," the child asked out of pure curiosity.

"There is something special about that glimmering hair of yours," Gothel started. "And I am going to figure out what it is."

"Oooh, a mystery," Rapunzel shouted excitedly as she jumped up and down.

She thought of all the stories her mother would tell her every night. She loved the ones with mysteries and clues. It made the gears in her small mind turn.

Rapunzel climbed into her mother's lap for a bedtime story. She loved it when her mother read her stories. It was like she jumped into another world when she heard them. Tonight was different, though; when the story came to an end, Rapunzel looked her mother in the eyes.

"Mama," she said. "Why do you get to leave the castle, and I cannot?"

"Baby, it is a cruel world out there. I do this for your protection. This is your special tower and your home, and I would do anything to keep you safe," she explained.

In all reality, Gothel was afraid Rapunzel's parents would find her and take her away. This would leave the woman with no one in the world. She couldn't bear the thought.

Rapunzel wrapped her arms around her mother and nuzzled into her shirt.

"Okay, Mama, I believe you," Rapunzel stuttered on her words. "I love that you keep me safe."

Mother Gothel melted over Rapunzel's words.

"I love you, Rapunzel," she said as she returned her daughter's hug.

"I love you too, Mama," Rapunzel squeaked as she kissed her mother on the cheek.

The world she was shielded from was not a bad world at all. Rapunzel had no other children to play with; she had only Mother Gothel. But she knew no better.

Mother Gothel tucked Rapunzel into her pink princess bed. When she was snuggled up tight, she kissed her on the forehead.

"Good night, my little bumble bee," she told her.

"Good night, mama," Rapunzel said in her small voice.

Rapunzel turned over in bed and fell asleep instantly.

As Mother Gothel stepped away from her bed. She found herself grateful that Rapunzel was a heavy sleeper. She knew she would sleep until at least Nine o'clock the next morning. The aging witch tip-toed down the stairs to the door of the castle. She closed the door quietly as she wandered off to Sapphire City. There, she would meet a trusted friend who might be able to tell her more about Rapunzel's hair.

Gothel traveled to her favorite pub, where she met up with an old friend. The woman who sat before her had lavendercolored skin and crazy black hair. Her name was Ursula.

"What did you want to meet me here for tonight," Ursula inquired.

"There is something peculiar about my child's hair," Gothel responded.

"All mothers think their child is special," Ursula snapped.

The young sea witch was still bitter over the kidnapping of her child.

"I know you are hurting, but I promise you I did not bring you over here over some bullshit," Gothel promised.

Ursula listened closely as she brought an onion ring to her mouth.

"Alright, let's hear it then," she said, feigning interest.

Ursula listened as Gothel spun her story. She told her about her glimmering hair in the moonlight and how no shears could cut it. Gothel had her mind set on learning the secrets of Rapunzel's hair.

"Wait a minute," Ursula interrupted. "How did you get the kid in the first place?"

Mother Gothel continued to weave the story of how things came to be the way they were. She told her of the love she had for her child and of the times they spent together. Ursula felt bad for the parents Gothel had hurt.

Ursula slammed her fist on the table. "You mean to tell me that you KIDNAPPED a child from her parents and kept her hidden away in a tower in fear of anyone finding her?" "Well.... Yes," Gothel murmured.

"How dare you come to me for help," she screamed at Mother Gothel.

Even if she did know the magic of Rapunzel's hair, there was no way Ursula was going to tell her now. Mother Gothel nearly spit her drink out. Her look darkened as she stared into her friend's eyes.

She stood up and stormed off from the table, leaving Ursula to pay the entire tab.

"The nerve of some people," Ursula said as she left the money on the table.

Mother Gothel walked into the night air and stumbled across a hole-in-the-wall store. When she stepped inside, the place seemed to be empty, but the glowing sign on the door said OPEN. The place was a total pigsty, but something in Gothel's gut told her that she would find exactly what she needed here.

The wiry-haired witch sifted through piles of dusty junk. She was surprised that no one had come out of the back to help her. After thirty minutes of searching, she stumbled upon a glowing book. The book was labeled *Everything Magical That Not Many Know.*

Gothel's eyes lit up as she flipped through the pages of the book. She looked for a store clerk but couldn't find one, so she left money on the counter and left the store. The morning was approaching, and the sun was beginning to rise; she needed a few hours of sleep before her beauty woke up.

When Mother Gothel arrived at the castle, she opened the door and snuck up the stairs. She peeked in at her daughter, who was still sound asleep. Gothel let out a sigh of relief to see her daughter in a deep slumber in her bed.

She lay on her pallet on the floor and drifted off to sleep. That early morning, she dreamed of Rapunzel as an adult. She saw herself climbing Rapunzel's hair to get into the tower. Gothel found it odd because there was a door to the tower.

Rapunzel woke her a few hours later, rubbing the sleep from her little eyes.

"Mama," she whispered into her mother's ear. "The sun is shining, the birds are chirping, a new day is here!"

"Good morning, my bumble bee," Mother Gothel said groggily.

"I'm hungry! Let's eat breakfast," Rapunzel chirped.

"Okay, baby. Breakfast it is."

Rapunzel's mouth watered as her mother prepared waffles and bacon for breakfast. When it was finished, the two of them ate together in the main room. Gothel saw changes in her daughter every day. She knew she had to implement some rules as Rapunzel grew older. Today, she would begin to teach her the things she would learn in school.

Mother Gothel taught her all about the stars in space and about math, science, and reading. Rapunzel loved the stars, and she loved to write everything down. Sometimes, her writing was barely legible, being that she was so small. But Mother Gothel was proud of her, nonetheless.

When the day was over and Rapunzel was tucked into bed, Mother Gothel sat down to read the book she had found in the shop. In the book, she read many odd things. She thumbed through the pages until the word "hair" caught her attention.

Her eyes scanned the page over and over again. What she found brought a dark smile to her face. Rapunzel was a powerful little girl, and the small girl did not know a thing about it. In the book, she read:

A child with hair that the moon has imbued has significant power. The hair of the child born with this hair is similar to the fountain of youth. When the child's hair is long enough, wrap the hair around you to wipe the signs of aging away.

This would be Mother Gothel's little secret. She had searched for years to find a way to remain young. She hated growing into a miserable hag. Wrinkles had started to form around her eyes and lips. More than anything, she wanted to be the young twenty-year-old witch she had been before she kidnapped Rapunzel. Thinking back on her youth, her demeanor darkened. Even though Rapunzel made her happy, she found herself lonely at times. Her parents had abandoned her when she was young, leaving her to fend for herself.

She stopped reading after she saw this, skipping the part about growing powers as the child ages. The power turns dark, to the likes of which Mother Gothel had never seen.

The aging witch fell asleep as she read, and before she knew it Rapunzel was at her side, tugging at her nightgown.

"It's time for school, Mama," she jumped up and down excitedly.

Rapunzel was excited to hear of the things she would learn all about. Mother Gothel taught Rapunzel different subjects and things about the world for four hours a day. She created homework for Rapunzel to complete, and they worked on it together. Mother Gothel took pride in how intelligent her daughter was.

Rapunzel had many books in her small room. Mother Gothel was adamant about her education. After school, Gothel would sit with her and have her read the many children's books she filled the tower with. They sat together on a large beanie chair and enjoyed each other's company as Rapunzel read.

After school every day, Mother Gothel taught her how to do her daily chores. Rapunzel was taught to dust everything in the tower she lived in and sweep the floors. Her mother told her she would teach her more as she got older.

Only after school, chores, and reading were done, Rapunzel was allowed to play. She didn't have many toys, but she enjoyed playing with her dolls and dressing up in princess clothing. She referred to a lot of the items in her small room as her friends. Rapunzel wished she had a real friend to talk to and play with, but she was perfectly content seeing only her mother every day.

The child had no idea what the world outside of the tower was like. She didn't care to know because she had been so sheltered her whole life.

Chapter Five

The Pains of Estrangement

As Rapunzel grew, her mother spent more and more time away from the castle, leaving Rapunzel with feelings of fear and abandonment. Rapunzel became a very solemn young girl who acted cheerful when her mother came home. She only came around three times a week to check on Rapunzel and stock the refrigerator with food.

The affection Rapunzel once received from Mother Gothel had deteriorated. Gothel hadn't told Rapunzel she loved her in over five years. Rapunzel learned to cook at an early age. She prepared herself breakfast, lunch, and dinner between learning and chores. At night, before she laid down to sleep, she prayed that her mother would love her again. She wanted nothing more than to spend time with her mother the way that they used to.

Rapunzel's hair now trailed behind her as she walked. When Mother Gothel came home one day, a smile crossed her face. "Hello, my little bumble bee," she said to Rapunzel.

"Hello, mama," Rapunzel replied, hoping her mother would hug her.

"I see your hair has grown very long," she said.

"Yes, mama, I take care of it every day. It takes me hours to comb the tangles out of my hair," she explained.

"Let me see," Mother Gothel reached out her hands.

Rapunzel walked toward her, tugging her hair from behind her and putting it over her shoulder to show it to her mother.

"So beautiful. May I," she reached to touch her daughter's hair.

"Of course, Mama," Rapunzel replied.

Mother Gothel took the hair in her hands and smiled. She began to wrap it around herself, leaving her daughter confused.

"What are you doing, Mama," Rapunzel asked nervously.

Mother Gothel spun around, wrapping herself completely in her daughter's hair. As she did so, Rapunzel watched her signs of aging disappear. Mother Gothel hugged Rapunzel's hair before detangling herself from it.

"Mama," Rapunzel started. "What happened?"

"Your hair is very powerful, my little bumble bee," Mother

Gothel explained. "You are a very, very special girl."
"Thank you, Mama," Rapunzel blushed.

Eight Years Later

Mother Gothel rarely came to see Rapunzel, and when she did, it was to wrap herself in her golden locks and erase any signs of aging. Rapunzel started to wonder if her mother even loved her anymore. They never spent time together the way they used to. The young woman spent most of her time alone, doing chores.

"Mama, why don't you stay for dinner," Rapunzel asked.

"Can't, got somewhere to be," Gothel barked at her as she put on a sleek, black dress.

"I thought the world was a scary place," Rapunzel said. "You certainly wouldn't be safe wearing anything like *that*."

"How dare you talk to me like that," Mother Gothel scorned her.

A look of pure shock crossed both of their faces as Mother Gothel's hand crashed into Rapunzel's face. She stared into her mother's eyes, still wondering what she did wrong. Rapunzel had just wondered why Gothel stayed away so often if the world was such a horrible place. Suddenly, Rapunzel couldn't wait for her mother to leave. Rapunzel ran off to her room, angry with the events that had just occurred. Her mother never laid a hand on her; this made her feel more alone and unloved than she ever had.

She heard her mother stomp down the stairs. She never dared to venture down there for fear of retaliation from her mother. Her whole life was spent on this floor in the tower that she cleaned every day. With her mother dressed like a whore, she knew the world was not a scary place.

In fact, it was a place to find attention, friends, and the love she had craved since she was a little girl. She dreamed of falling in love with a prince, like the princesses in her stories. But she knew that could never be.

Rapunzel was so angry and beside herself that she punched a hole in her wall. As the rage consumed her, she watched as her hair turned a deep black color. She wondered what this meant, but she brushed it off, making plans for the following day.

When night fell, Rapunzel lay in bed tossing and turning. When she drifted off to sleep, she dreamt of anger and violence. She saw her black hair in her dreams; it had an ominous glow. She watched as her hair absorbed a man whole, and she woke in a cold sweat.

It was early morning when she woke, and she had no intention of doing any of her chores today. She was still angry that her mother had hit her, and she hoped she wouldn't see her again for a long time.

Rapunzel had counted her birthdays from the position of the stars she watched in her telescope. She was eighteen now and plenty old enough to be on her own. The young woman spent three hours coming through her thick, black hair. Her black hair reminded her of her mother, and this made her even more angry.

The young woman spent the better half of the day lounging around and eating snacks. As she sat there, she read her favorite book on astrology. Rapunzel learned that she was a Sagittarius. The thought of horoscopes, planets, and the signs they were aligned in intrigued her.

Rapunzel dug through the closet of clothes her mother kept in an armoire. She was told never to step foot in her mother's room, but today, she didn't care. The young woman shuffled through the many dresses in her mother's armoire in search of the perfect one.

Her eyes lit up as her fingers grazed the perfect silk dress. It would accent her curves perfectly, and it was her favorite color: Emerald Green. Green, like a set of eyes she remembers looking into as a baby. She couldn't remember the face, but oh, she remembered the eyes. The kind of eyes that poured pure love into her soul. It was a woman's eyes, but who was the woman?

Rapunzel removed the dress from the hanger. As she was leaving the room, she found a beautiful diamond-studded headband. She grabbed it and scurried off to her room. In the safety of her own room, she changed from her pajamas into a beautiful silk dress. The silk felt like heaven on her skin, and she felt sexy, confident, and proud of the woman she was.

Rapunzel gazed into the full-length mirror on her wall. Her hair shone with a brightness she had never seen before. The diamonds in her hair were accentuated by the deep black color of her hair. They sparkled brightly in the moonlight poured in through the window. *Her hair was truly a wonder to behold.*

She ventured to the window she gazed out of every day; her thoughts were set on leaving the tower today. She would sneak out; Mother Gothel would never know. Rapunzel smiled as she formed the plan in her mind.

She knew the risk she was taking, and she feared getting lost. But she felt trapped from being confined to a tower for the entire eighteen years of her existence. Rapunzel lifted the hem of her dress and crept down the stairs of the tower. When she reached the bottom, she found herself in front of a large wooden door.

She pushed the door open, and a fresh burst of autumn air caressed her cheeks. Rapunzel took a deep breath, nervous to take her first step outside. As she did, she felt the grass between her toes. This was a new sensation. One that she had never felt in her life. Rapunzel wiggled her toes in the grass, giggling as it tickled her soles.

The young girl wandered toward the large pear tree that she always stared at from the castle window. She reached up for a branch and picked a pear; Rapunzel slid down against the tree's trunk and sat on the ground eating her fruit.

The peace left her quickly; she was suddenly filled with fear and anxiety. She heard noises she was unfamiliar with, and she could feel eyes boring into her. Being alone in the darkness of night made her nervous. Rapunzel rushed back to the tower and ran up the stairs. The young girl didn't realize she tracked grass and mud behind her. She jumped in the shower, got dressed for bed, and started to comb her hair. Within an hour, she was lying in bed pretending to sleep, just in case Gothel returned home to check on her.

Rapunzel stirred in her bed when she heard the door downstairs close. She heard Gothel creeping up the steps and got up to check on her. The young girl rose from her bed to check on her mother. As she left her room, she bumped into Mother Gothel.

"Your hair," Gothel stared at Rapunzel.

"What about it," Rapunzel said, forgetting her hair was now black.

"Why is your hair black," Gothel asked her.

"Oh, um... I don't know. It just changed," she replied.

"What are you doing here," Rapunzel asked her mother.

"I forgot something, my dear. Please go back to bed," Gothel responded.

"Yes, mother," Rapunzel responded.

Rapunzel went back into her room, waiting for Mother Gothel's door to shut. She closed her door, leaving it cracked so she could spy on her mother. She shied away from the door so her mother couldn't see her. When she heard Gothel pass by, she peeked out of the door. In her hand, she had a whip, handcuffs, and other strange accessories that Rapunzel had never seen before.

Rapunzel lay in her bed as she heard her mother drop everything she had.

"RAPUNZEL," she heard her mother yell out.

Rapunzel stepped out of her door, worried about what her mother might say.

"Yes, mama," Rapunzel asked sheepishly.

"What the hell is all of this," Gothel pointed to the mud and grass that was tracked up the stairs to the castle.

"Did you track in some dirt, Mom," Rapunzel replied.

"You left the castle, didn't you," Gothel spat. "You will rue this day. As I leave here tonight, the door will be removed, and you will be sealed in this castle. When I come to the window, I will call to you and climb up that beautiful hair of yours."

Gothel grabbed her things, along with boards, nails, and a hammer. She then stormed down the steps to the door and slammed it on her way out. Rapunzel could hear her mother prying the door off its hinges and hammering the boards in place.

Rapunzel sobbed at the thought of being a prisoner in her own home. She was her mother's captive, and life was very unfair. What was so scary about the world that required her to be locked up while Gothel ran all over town?

The young woman ran off to bed, covering her eyes to catch her tears. After hours of crying, she drifted off to sleep. She dreamt of lonely times that evening, saddening her further.

Would she ever find true love? Or was she destined to become a Lonely old hag?

Chapter Six

Gothel's Night Out

Mother Gothel was out of breath by the time she made it down the stairs of the tower. She was frustrated that Rapunzel had gone against her wishes and was set on making sure it would never happen again. She set her supplies on the ground and placed her other things on the other side of her.

Gothel grabbed the hammer and started to pry the door away from the hinges. She didn't realize how much strength she had lost over the years. Yet, her anger allowed her to rip the door off the hinges and throw it aside.

Once the door was on the ground behind her, she lifted a board and nailed it in place. She repeated this board by board until the entrance was permanently blocked. As much of an inconvenience as this was for her, she was glad Rapunzel could no longer escape the tower. When Gothel was pleased with her work, she picked up the things she originally left the house with and wandered toward Sapphire City.

Gothel held her toys close as she wandered through the forest. She had a sexy night planned for her and her sex slave. They had booked a room at a fancy hotel on the other end of the city. Her heart raced as she approached the city's center. He was waiting for her, and it had been forever since she had felt a man's touch.

She stopped at a shop and grabbed lingerie she knew he would like. On her way out, she turned left and bumped into Ursula, who shot her a dirty look and rushed off in the opposite direction. After ten minutes of walking, Gothel arrived at the front of the ten-story building.

It was late November, and Gothel was shopping for Rapunzel. The Holiday season was looming, and she had no idea what to buy for her daughter. As she entered a small shop, there stood a small man. What drew Gothel in was his likeness to an elf. His golden locks and pointed ears stirred her bits in ways they had never felt. She fell into his beady eyes, and that's when she knew she had to have him now.

Gothel snapped out of her daydream. She pushed the large glass doors open and stepped into a lavish lobby. It was adorned with long strands of gold upon deep red walls. Some candles lined the walls; they led to the elevators.

Rumpelstiltskin was his name. He told her they would be staying on the third floor this evening. Her heart pounded in her chest as she remembered his words. "Get ready for the time of your life," he had whispered to her. She was excited at the thought of being in control. Nothing turned her on more.

Gothel felt her sex throbbing in anticipation. She pushed the button on the elevator, and the third door opened seconds later. When she stepped onto the elevator, she clutched her arsenal of sex toys close to her chest.

As the doors to the elevator opened to the third floor of the hotel, Gothel's breath was taken away by the rose petals leading down the hall. She knew Rumpelstiltskin loved sex, but she had no idea he was a romantic man. Gothel followed the rose petals and arrived at the room where her sex slave was waiting for her.

The door was slightly ajar when she arrived. She peeked through the crack of the door to see Rumpelstiltskin lying on the bed with his dick standing at attention. Gothel pushed the door open and laid her eyes upon her most favored new toy, Rumpelstiltskin.

"Hello, beautiful," Rumpel greeted her.

"Hello, slave," she replied, her eyes turning dark.

"I have never heard sexier words," Rumpel winked at her.

"Shut up," Gothel commanded.

She watched as Rumpelstiltskin pinched his forefinger and thumb together and brushed them across his lips, showing her his lips were sealed. Gothel approached her slave and placed her tools on the bed.

Gothel began to sway her hips as she walked to his side. She leaned over and planted a kiss on his smooth lips. She reached for the handcuffs at the end of the bed. She had brought two sets with her; she locked one cuff of each set around both of his hands. She continued by locking his arms to the bars of the bed.

She danced for her slave. Her moves were sultry and smooth. Gothel slowly removed her dress to reveal the lingerie she had purchased on her way here. She pretended to drop something and bent over, listening to Rumpel tug at the cuffs attempting to touch her ass.

"Uh, Uh, Uh," Gothel said as she turned around.

Rumpel's lustful glare followed her to the foot of the bed, where she grabbed a length of rope she had placed on the trunk in front of the bed. Gothel tied the rope to his feet and spread them apart, tying each foot to bars on the bottom of the bed.

Once his hands and feet were secured, she grabbed the flogger she held tightly to on the way to the room. She watched as Rumpel's eyes widened in excitement.

"Are you ready, slave," she asked Rumpel.

Rumpel nodded his head frantically in anticipation. He groaned as he waited for his punishment.

Gothel dropped the tails of the flogger onto his skin and let them drag across the length of his body. She listened to him squirm and smiled. Gothel raised the flogger in the air and thrashed it against her lover's torso.

She watched as his chest rose into the air, and she heard a low growl come from his body. After a few thrashes, Rumpel was nearly drooling. Gothel placed her hands at his ankles, and with the lightest touch, she slid her hands up Rumpelstiltskin's thin, bony legs. The witch could feel her slave shiver as she continued to caress his body.

Rumpel's eyes were glued to Gothel. He waited in anticipation as her mouth got closer to his rock-hard erection. She heard him whimper as she hovered above him. Gothel brought her mouth to his inner thighs and massaged each of them with her tongue before teasing his cock with her lips.

"Please," Rumpel whined.

Gothel shot him a dirty look as she squeezed his testicles.

"Shut it, slave," she said darkly. "Everything happens on my time."

"Yes, Ma'am," Rumpel nodded.

TANGLED DISASTERS

Gothel moved her silky hand around his shaft. She could hear a sharp intake of his breath as she placed her lips on the head of his erection. He knew better than to move or make a noise, so he stayed perfectly still.

Gothel swirled and flicked her tongue around the tip of his dick. When he least expected it, she took the entire length of him into her mouth and down her throat. She continued her assault as she moved him in and out of her mouth, using her lips and teeth to make it an extra sensual experience. When she felt him truly enjoying himself, she inserted her finger into his ass.

She could feel him about to explode in ecstasy. She took her mouth off him and released the pressure of her hand. Gothel felt his body slump in disappointment.

"Just wait, my love," she cooed at her slave. "You will enjoy what is coming next."

Rumpel just stared up at her with longing eyes.

"It's my turn," she said seductively.

Gothel climbed up his body and hovered over him so her pussy was dangling over his face.

"Are you ready for me," she asked him.

"Yes, master, more than you know," he breathed.

"Show me your magic, Rumpel," she giggled, her clit throbbing at this point.

Gothel could hear him tugging at his restraints, which only turned her on more.

"Oh, I suppose I can let your hands be free for this one," she laughed.

Gothel released his hands from the cuffs. Rumpel's hands flew to her hips as he pulled her down on his face. Her juices dripped all over his face as his tongue licked and flicked her clit. She threw her head back in pleasure as Rumpel continued to work his magic. Gothel's breath caught as he felt his tongue enter her entrance; he brought his hand up to her sex and used his finger to circle her clit as he moved his tongue in and out of her pussy.

An electric shock jolted through Rumpel as he felt her sex lock around his tongue. She screamed out in ecstasy as the first of many orgasms took hold of her. Her fluids were like sweet nectar from the gods; he slurped up every drop. "OH," she yelled out. "You are a god, Rumpel." "A god to my goddess," Rumpel replied.

"Are you in for the fucking of your life," Gothel asked her slave.

"As in as I will ever be," Rumpel let out a hearty laugh.

Gothel slid her body down his torso, stopping to kiss him deeply as she pushed herself onto his erection. She could feel his dick grow even harder inside of her. Gothel rode him so hard she could hardly breathe. She leaned over and took his hair in her hands, and forced his lips to hers. He pounded into her repeatedly and felt her pussy lock around him again as they both experienced an earth-shattering orgasm.

The screams of both lovers could be heard clearly across the third floor of the hotel. Gothel released Rumpel's remaining limbs from the cuffs and lay beside him. Once she was lying beside him, they were face to face, looking into each other's eyes.

"The sparkle in your eye is forever imprinted in my mind," Rumpel whispered in her ear.

Gothel leaned forward and planted a soft kiss on his lips. The way this night went, she knew she would be back for more. He was quickly becoming an addiction she had no intention of kicking.

"Lay flat on your stomach," Rumpel told her. He could feel the questioning in her body. "Trust me, you are going to love what comes next."

Gothel complied and rolled over onto her stomach. She rested her head on the pillows as she felt Rumpel trace loving patterns down her spine with his fingers. Once he reached her ass, he raised his hand in the air and gave her cheeks a hard slap. He could feel her jump in surprise as he did so.

"This is just the beginning," he giggled.

Gothel shivered as she felt his finger slide between her ass cheeks. She groaned as she felt him bury his face in her ass. He spread her cheeks apart and began to tease her anus with his tongue. The swirling and twirling of his tongue left Gothel on cloud nine. She moaned in pleasure as he stuck his tongue into her asshole.

"You taste so sweet," he said.

He continued to eat her as he slid two fingers into her pussy. He curled them in such a way that they hit her G-Spot as he circled her clit with his thumb. It wasn't long before she was screaming his name and her pussy locked around his fingers.

At this point, Rumpel was rock hard again and ready to bury his dick so far up her ass that she wouldn't remember his name.

"Tonight, you will take every inch of me, in each and every hole," he smiled darkly.

"I love the sound of that," Gothel breathed.

The witch braced herself as she felt Rumpelstiltskin's hands caressing her ass. He rubbed both cheeks, continuing by spreading them apart. Gothel cried out as he slammed into her ass. The feeling was so divine that she pushed herself back into him as he thrust.

Gothel listened to him shuffle as he thrust.

"I have a surprise for you," he chuckled.

"I love surprises; give me everything you've got," Gothel moaned as he shifted.

Rumpelstiltskin pulled a vibrator from the post of the bed.

"Here you go," he breathed as he pushed the vibrator into her entrance.

"OH," he heard her cry out as he continued to thrust.

"You feel so good," he growled.

Rumpel continued to pound into her as she cried out in pleasure. Her sensitive clit and entrance were throbbing, and another orgasm was building. Rumpel caressed her ass as he thrusted, and he felt her body tense as another orgasm hit her.

"I hope this won't be our last time," Gothel said as she turned over.

"I can never get enough of you," Rumpel whispered in her ear.

Rumpelstiltskin pulled out of her and wandered toward the bathroom at the other end of the room. There, he warmed a rag for Gothel and returned to clean her up before cleaning himself off.

"You are so attentive," Gothel said in amazement.

"Only for you, my love," he said.

The two of them found their clothes and got dressed. Rumpelstiltskin kissed Gothel deeply before leaving the room.

She was sad to see him go, but she realized she should check on Rapunzel with the recent trouble they had. Gothel dropped the key card on the counter before leaving the room. She rushed out of the hotel and into the night to head back to the tower.

Chapter Seven

Let Down Your Long Hair

As Gothel made it into the woods, she picked up her pace. She was nervous about Rapunzel's whereabouts. This was until she realized that she had closed off the entrance. She didn't see Rapunzel as the type to break free.

When she reached the tower, she spotted Rapunzel awake, staring at the moon from her window. She was stroking the hair on her scalp with her hands; it was shimmering in the light of the full moon. Gothel trotted to the window and stood underneath. Rapunzel hadn't heard her, so she shouted up to her.

"Rapunzel, Rapunzel, let down your long hair!"

Startled, Rapunzel looked down at her mother. She was worried that she would be angry that she was still awake. She shook this thought from her head, though. She was eighteen, and she would stay up as late as she damn well pleased.

"My hair," Rapunzel asked, confused.

"Yes, my child, your hair!" she called back up to her.

Rapunzel started to gather her long hair from behind her. Luckily for her mother, she had tied it into a ponytail earlier that day. The young woman threw her long locks out of the window, worried that something might happen when her mother tried to climb it.

Rapunzel felt Gothel pull and tug at her hair. After several minutes, her mother had climbed up her hair, and Rapunzel was helping her through the window.

"Hello, Mother," Rapunzel greeted her.

"Hi, Rapunzel," Gothel said curtly. "Why are you still awake?"

"I can't sleep; the full moon always keeps me awake, mama," Rapunzel whined sleepily.

"Oh, right," Gothel muttered. "I forgot."

Gothel shuffled off to her bedroom. She pushed the door open and sensed something different. She searched her room for anything missing but couldn't place her finger on what it was. The witch gathered a towel and her pajamas and tip-toed to the bathroom, where she started the shower.

The feeling of the steam hitting her face somehow brought back memories of the evening she had just shared with her lover. Gothel stripped down and got into the shower. She leaned her head back, letting the hot water soak her hair. As water ran down her body, she found her hand traveling toward her clit.

She moaned before her hand ever hit, still feeling Rumpel inside of her. Her fingers found her sweet spot, and she circled it roughly. She struggled to keep her noise to a minimal level as she inserted her fingers into her entrance. Within minutes, an orgasm hit, and her pussy tightened around her fingers.

She washed her body after this and shampooed her hair.

Gothel turned the knobs to the shower and turned the water off. The aging witch snatched the towel off the sink when she brought it to her body, she noticed wrinkles on her hand.

Her mind flew back to the fountain of youth Rapunzel had for hair. She grinned, thinking of how young she would look when she wrapped herself up in her daughter's hair. Gothel slid her pajamas on and left her room. When she stepped into the main room, she noticed Rapunzel was back at the window, staring at the moon.

"Rapunzel," she said softly. "Is there anything I can do to help you sleep?"

"Can we drink hot cocoa together, mama," Rapunzel raised her clasped hands in the air.

"Ok, darling. Hot chocolate it is," Gothel sighed.

She watched as her daughter's eyes lit up, and she left the room to heat water for their late-night hot chocolate. When she returned to the room, Rapunzel had pulled out two bean bag chairs and placed them in the center of the room, where the moon shone brightly on them.

Gothel walked into the room and handed a mug of steaming cocoa to her daughter. She wandered to the bean bag chair and sat down.

"Mm, marshmallows," Rapunzel said excitedly. "You always did make the best hot chocolate."

Gothel looked over to see a big smile on her daughter's face. For the first time in a long time, Rapunzel's smile warmed the witch's heart. Gothel watched as Rapunzel yawned after her hot cocoa.

"Why don't you try and get some sleep," Gothel said sweetly.

"I think I will," Rapunzel replied.

The young lady rose from her bean bag chair and headed to the kitchen. She placed her cup in the sink and then walked to her bedroom, where she lay in bed and instantly fell asleep.

The Next Morning...

Rapunzel woke early the next morning. She left her room for breakfast and realized that her mother was nowhere to be found. The thought of this excited her; she had to figure out a way out of this tower, or rather, she had to have someone come to spend time with her. Rapunzel mulled her thoughts over for quite some time. Something brought her to the large window of the main room.

Rapunzel stared out the window into the autumn sunlight. The colorful falling leaves always fascinated her; this was her favorite time of the year. The sun was peeking over the horizon, leaving the land with a brilliant glow. There was something magical about this time of the day. It seemed to wash all her troubles away, if only for a moment.

After watching the sunrise, Rapunzel wandered off to her mother's room. If she was going to get anyone's attention, she would have to look beautiful. The young lady shuffled through her mother's dresses. Deep in the back of the closet, she found a silky black gown. It was perfect for grabbing the attention of any man that crossed her path.

Rapunzel combed her hair for hours; she managed to braid the entirety of it. Back in her mother's bedroom, she started to look through her mother's cosmetics. She powdered her face, painted her cheeks rosy with blush, and colored her lips with deep red lipstick. As she put the lipstick down, she noticed a palette of myriad colors of eyeshadow. She chose a glimmering golden color to put on her eyelids and finished her look with deep black mascara.

When Rapunzel looked in the mirror, she saw not the little girl she had always known but a grown woman staring back at her. A grown woman starving for the touch of a man, as she had read in many of the books she snuck from her mother's room. "Something More" was her favorite.

The young woman walked back out into the main room and stood in front of the window. Not many men crossed this part of the forest, but Rapunzel was hopeful. An idea struck her

when she peered into the distance. Rapunzel started to sing.

The sound that came from her lips was intoxicating.

As she sang, she saw a young man step out of the thicker part of the forest. His face was chiseled, and he had sandy blonde hair. He looked strong but reserved, and his eyes were sapphire blue. Rapunzel instantly desired him as if she were under a spell. She kept singing her song, and the man walked closer and closer to the tower in search of the source of the beautiful voice he was hearing.

When the young man was just below the window, Rapunzel looked down and shouted.

"Hey, up here!"

The young man looked up, and a lustful gaze filled his eyes.

"Well, hello there," he said, winking at Rapunzel.

The sparkle in her eyes stirred something in his pants.

"Would you like to come up here," Rapunzel asked.

"I'm Fernando," he introduced himself.

"Rapunzel," pleased to meet you, she curtsied through the window.

"How do you propose I get up there," Fernando asked out of curiosity.

Rapunzel lifted her long, braided hair and threw it out of the window.

"Climb my hair," Rapunzel shouted.

"Won't it hurt," he asked.

"No, I'll be fine," Rapunzel assured him.

Rapunzel watched as Fernando grabbed her hair. His strong arms helped him to climb quickly and effortlessly. Once he reached the top, he looked into Rapunzel's eyes. He climbed through the window and stood on his feet.

"You are...stunning," Fernando told her as he stood before her.

Rapunzel turned deep red. "Thank you. You aren't so bad yourself, champ."

They laughed together as he reached for Rapunzel's hand. She grabbed his hand and led him to her bedroom. He couldn't help but stare at her ass as he followed her. When they reached the bed, Rapunzel pushed Fernando onto it.

"I am new at this. Do you mind showing me the ropes," she smiled meekly at Fernando.

As she said this, she raised a set of ropes in her hands.

"New, huh," Fernando chuckled.

"Maybe I lied," she winked at him.

Rapunzel lifted Fernando's arms and tied his hands to her bedpost. She heard his breath catch as she tied the rope tight. Underneath her, she felt his dick harden in his pants. She grinded against him, groaning as she did so. Reaching beside her, she produced more rope. Before she tied it around each leg, she removed his pants and boxers.

"Standing at attention for me, baby, I love it," she whispered in his ear.

She heard him tugging at the bedpost and wanted to take him then and there. But she had to make him wait, to make him suffer and work for what he wanted. She slowly lifted herself from lying on top of him and ripped his shirt off.

"Oh, look at those abs; I could eat them up," she said as she looked him up and down.

He stared down at her longingly. Rapunzel giggled as she saw the want in his eyes. She began to strip, slowly unbuttoning the dress and letting it drop to the floor. Fernando's jaw dropped open as he watched her perky breasts bounce in her bra. Rapunzel reached behind her back and unclasped her bra, freeing her breasts from their homely prison. She turned around, bending over as she removed her panties.

She could feel his eyes on her, and nothing turned her on more. Rapunzel stood up slowly and turned around. When she glanced at Fernando, he was entranced by her curves and licking his lips.

"Come on, Baby," Fernando said, his voice laced with need.

"Just a minute," Rapunzel replied as she walked away.

When Rapunzel returned, she held a flogger in her hands.

"I am low on supplies," she whispered. "But I will make this worth your while."

Rapunzel winked at Fernando as she slowly approached him.

"Be gentle," Fernando said. "I have never been with a woman in this way."

"Oh," Rapunzel smiled darkly. "I have zero intentions of being gentle with you; I will show you the fine line between pain and pure pleasure. Do you trust me?"

"How can I not trust a fine woman like you with all of your delicious curves," he breathed.

Rapunzel raised the flogger in the air; Fernando took a deep breath as the flogger's tails thrashed into his body. She thrashed him a few times before stroking his stomach with her hands.

"How did that feel, handsome," Rapunzel ran her fingers up his thighs. She could feel him pushing himself toward her, wanting her more than ever.

"I wasn't expecting it...to feel so divine," he admitted.

Rapunzel chuckled as she climbed on top of him. The feeling of the two of them being skin-to-skin was the most arousing thing Rapunzel had felt in her life. She planted soft kisses down his chest to his groin.

"Are you ready for me," she asked him.

"You have no idea," he chuckled.

Rapunzel slid down, leaving her mouth hovering over his rock-hard dick. She grabbed the base of it and licked it like a lollipop. She smiled as he shivered, a chill running up his spine. Fernando's breath caught in his throat as she took his entire dick into her throat. She moved with such finesse that his legs were shaking in pleasure. She took him out of her mouth right as he was ready to bust.

Rapunzel moved upward, releasing his hands from the restraints.

"It's your turn now," Rapunzel said seductively as she climbed further up his chest. "Eat your heart out."

Fernando blushed as she said this. He grabbed her and pulled her dripping-wet pussy over his face. His thumb found her clit like a bee to honey, and he circled it roughly, causing her to moan in pleasure. The assault continued when he pushed his tongue into her entrance, licking up every drop of her juices it could find. He could feel her grinding against his tongue.

He grabbed her hips and lifted her up. "Release my feet," he said gently.

Rapunzel reached back and untied the ropes from his ankles. Fernando then grabbed her and placed her on the bed, so he was on top of her. He trailed soft kisses down her abdomen and worked his way down until his face was hovering near her groin.

Fernando inserted two fingers into her dripping entrance and one into her ass. He curved the two fingers in her pussy in such a way that he hit the right spot, causing Rapunzel to tense in response. She grabbed handfuls of his hair and pulled his face in closer to him. He hovered there for a moment, allowing the heat of his breath to make her clit throb even more. When he felt she couldn't wait any longer, he shoved his face into her, flicking and licking her clit; he could feel her melting all around him.

Rapunzel's pussy clamped and locked around his fingers as she reached her climax. Fernando looked up at her and smiled.

"I'm not done with you yet," he winked.

Fernando shifted upward, bringing Rapunzel's legs up over his shoulders. He lined his dick up with her entrance and thrust into her without hesitation. Rapunzel gasped as he did so. Traces of blood-tinged fluids stained the sheets below her. A man had never touched her, but she had read all about it in the books in her mother's room. "The Fourth Base Dungeon" taught her quite a bit about the sex lifestyle she was interested in.

Fernando repeatedly slammed into her, both sharing sounds of ecstasy in each movement. Rapunzel gazed into his eyes as he pumped the last few times; she locked around him again, soaking up every bit of cum as he busted inside of her.

"So, you were new at this," Fernando chuckled as he looked down at the sheets.

"Oops," Rapunzel blushed.

Fernando brought her legs down and allowed them to fall onto the mattress. He leaned on top of her, kissing her deeply.

"You are the best-tasting virgin I have ever had the pleasure of knowing," he told her. "I better get going. Should we meet again, beautiful?"

"Uhmmm," Rapunzel hesitated.

He climbed off her and gathered his clothes. Rapunzel eyed him up and down as he dressed, trying to soak in every inch of his body before he disappeared. She doubted he would return.

Chapter Eight

Mother Knows Best

Rapunzel rushed around her room, cleaning up any evidence of her loss of innocence. Gothel would bubble with rage if she knew that Rapunzel had let someone into the tower. She had a niggling feeling that Gothel would be able to figure it out somehow. This was a worry for another time; she needed to focus on the now. The young girl felt like her mother was trying to keep her from the world. She wasn't a trophy to be stored but a fine wine to be tasted and revered.

Right as the sheet finished burning in the fireplace, Rapunzel heard a familiar voice calling to her from the window. "Rapunzel, let down your hair," Gothel called to her.

"Yes, mama, be right there," Rapunzel hollered back.

She rushed to remake her bed and put Gothel's flogger and ropes back where they belonged. Rapunzel then made her way to the window, where she tossed her long locks over the edge of the sill. Her face twisted as her mother tugged at her hair. Gothel always took forever to climb up to the tower; Rapunzel always grew bored of waiting for her to make it to the window.

Rapunzel tugged her mother over the edge of the window, and she came crashing into the floor. Rapunzel was taken aback by how old and feeble her mother looked. Her skin was thin on her hands, her hair was graying, and lines adorned the corners of her mouth and eyes.

"Hello, my beauty," Gothel's voice cracked as she spoke.

"Hello, mother," Rapunzel gasped.

"What happened to me," Gothel asked, as her hands shook in front of her eyes. "I didn't look like this when I started climbing."

Gothel tried to stand but felt she was too weak. Rapunzel helped her up and walked her to her bed. Gothel slept for days after Rapunzel laid her in bed. She was beginning to worry, but Gothel climbed out of bed and somehow looked younger than she had been the other day.

"Good morning, child," Gothel said, avoiding Rapunzel's hair like the plague.

"How are you feeling, mother," Rapunzel asked, concerned.

"I might ask the same of you," Gothel said accusingly.

She stared her daughter in the eyes. Rapunzel looked like a deer in headlights.

"Whatever do you mean, mother," she asked.

"Something is different about you; I haven't put my finger on it yet," Gothel said sternly. "I will figure it out, whether you tell me or not."

Rapunzel felt as though she was found out but continued to play dumb. She would never admit outright to her mother that she had had a man in the tower. A stranger, one that she had slept with. She was no longer chaste. Her forbidden fruit had been tasted—tainted.

She was more of a woman than she was before; she felt different. But, at the same time, she felt the same.

Rapunzel's conscience screamed at her to be honest with her mother, but she knew that could never happen. It would be the end of the small amount of freedom she had ever had. This had to remain her secret until she was found out.

"You were gone for so long, Mother," Rapunzel pouted, trying to redirect her mother's attention.

"Don't play coy with me, girl," Gothel snapped.

Gothel began to search the tower. Hoping to find some clue as to what was so different about Rapunzel. It was right under her nose, but somehow it was untraceable. Her eyes shot over to the fireplace. It contained far more soot and ash than usual.

"What have you been burning, Rapunzel," she asked. "We don't have any logs, although we do need some, so tell me, what have you been burning?"

Rapunzel broke her gaze from her mother's eyes, looking at the ground.

"I haven't been burning anything," Rapunzel lied.

"You always were a terrible liar. Now, tell me the truth, or there will be consequences," Gothel spoke.

"I am stuck in the same tower I always have been, how could I do anything that would upset you? I clean and study all day, and I often look to the stars as an escape from my miserable existence," Rapunzel sighed.

"Miserable?" Gothel yelled. "You're safe from the cruel world inside of a tower where you have EVERYTHING you need! And you are miserable," she spat.

"I yearn for more in life, more than being a prisoner locked away in a tower by her own *mother*," Rapunzel snapped.

Gothel shut down. She knew Rapunzel was right in what she was saying and could not think of a clever enough response to de-escalate the situation. She stared at the floor, tapping her foot.

"You used this as a deflection. You need to answer me when I speak to you! What has been happening in this tower," She yelled, veins popping out of her temples.

Rapunzel's hair started to move on its own. Her locks looked like tendrils, ready to attack their prey. Only her mother was the prey. She tried to will her hair to relax, but it wouldn't work.

"How could you attack your own mother, the one who loved and cared for you since the day you were born," Gothel cried.

"It's not me, it's my hair. I can't control it," Rapunzel fibbed.

At first, she didn't have control, but she figured it out quickly.

The power came naturally.

"I'm sorry, Rapunzel," Gothel pleaded. "I'll no longer elicit the truth you work so hard to hide."

Rapunzel's hair began to settle. The rage she felt inside of her simmered down, and she started to think about what she almost did. The raven-haired young woman was beginning to scare herself, but she knew Gothel had done wrong by her many times, even in ways she was unaware of.

Was Gothel even her real mother? They looked nothing alike.

"I will have to bring someone here to meet you, someone to tame that wild hair of yours," Gothel muttered as she tied the sheets together.

"What do you mean, tame?" Rapunzel asked.

"Rumpelstiltskin would love to meet someone like you," Gothel cackled.

"Rumpel-who?" Rapunzel asked.

Gothel backed away, tying the sheets to a pillar in the main room. Rapunzel watched as she tossed the sheets over the edge of the sill and made her way down the tower's side.

Plots of revenge began to form in the young girl's mind. Rapunzel would find justice for her mother's misdeeds, even if her hair were a weapon she would use against Gothel. The expression on Rapunzel's face darkened as she plotted against the woman who raised her.

Rapunzel drifted off to sleep quickly that night. The argument with her mother had taken a toll on her. That night, she dreamed of the emerald eyes she had seen somewhere before. They were kind eyes that she couldn't place. *Who could this mystery person be?*

Later that evening

Gothel met Rumpelstiltskin at the same hotel they had rendezvoused earlier in the week. This time, they met in the hotel's conference room to discuss the matter of Rapunzel. Gothel expressed the dangers posed by Rapunzel if her hair were to touch another life.

"Rumpel, is there anything we can do with that feral hair of hers?" she pleaded.

Rumpelstiltskin placed his finger on his chin and tapped it.

"Hmm, I do have some ideas. You will have to show me how bad you want them," Rumpel winked at his lover.

Gothel giggled in excitement. "I've never heard sexier words," she said seductively.

Rumpel approached Gothel and brushed her hand with his fingers, sending tingles up her spine. It was almost magical how he could turn her on with one simple touch. One simple look, even. Gothel just wanted this to be fun, but she found herself falling in love, as she feared.

She took his hand in hers and led him out of the conference room. The two lovers stopped at the counter and paid for a room. Until this evening, Gothel had no idea of Rumpelstiltskin's secrets.

As they walked down the hall on the third floor to their room, she noticed rose petals appearing out of thin air. Gothel gasped.

"You have magic, too," she breathed.

"Too," Rumpel asked curiously.

"It seems we both have our secrets; now we have another shared bond," Gothel said as she squeezed his hand.

Rumpel pushed the door open to their room. As the door opened, the room smelled of vanilla and roses. There were candles lit all over the room, and the bed was adorned with silk sheets and fluffy pillows.

Gothel ran to the bed and hopped in, rolling around like a small child. Rumpel's eyes lit up as he watched her roll around. When he knew it was safe, he jumped in beside her. They laughed together for a few minutes before Rumpel leaned in and pressed his soft lips into hers.

It had felt like forever since they had last been together, and the fire raging in both of their souls had both Gothel and Rumpel restless and full of need. Gothel wrapped her legs around Rumpelstiltskin as she kissed him deeply. Rumpel wrapped his arms around her and kissed her forehead. A more profound connection formed between them as they lay there staring into each other's eyes.

"I need you," Gothel whispered in his ear.

"I'm right here," Rumpel said lovingly as he ran his fingers through her hair.

Gothel ran her hand down Rumpel's chest until she hit his groin. He was already standing at attention for her, and this made her bits dripping wet. The small man reached over to the nightstand, where he produced handcuffs.

Rumpel grabbed Gothel's hands and cuffed them to the bars on the headboard of the bed. He heard her breath catch as he hovered over her, gazing into her eyes. He caressed her cheek with the back of his hand before he began to trail many soft kisses down her neck to her chest. He sucked on her nipples and grazed each with his teeth, making them stand erect.

He hovered above her and admired her delicious curves, then continued kissing her all the way down to her sex. Rumple then raised his hand in the air and produced a vibrating anal plug. Gothel shivered with excitement. Rumpel took the plug in his mouth and licked all around it before filling her asshole with heavenly vibrations.

He heard her groan as she tugged at the restraints, wishing she could wrap her fingers in his soft hair. Rumpel's hand rose into the air again, this time producing a riding crop.

"Tsk, Tsk, my love. You are a naughty girl," he growled as he sat up.

Gothel's eyes widened as the crop came crashing into her abdomen. With each strike he caressed the beautiful pink skin with his soft hands. This left Gothel's clit throbbing. She needed him now more than ever.

Rumpel traced intricate patterns down Gothel's abdomen before he inserted two fingers into her sex. He then leaned down and hovered over her, breathing on her clit. To Gothel, it was an eternity before his tongue ever reached her most sensitive parts.

Her lover swirled his tongue around her clit, sucking on it as he worked his magic. Within seconds, Gothel felt an orgasm building. With his free hand, he lashed her with the crop again, causing her to explode in ecstasy—leaving him to clean up every drop of pussy juice that poured from her bits.

"Oh," she yelled. "You are a god."

Rumpel climbed on top of her, his rock-hard dick waving in front of her mouth. Rapunzel opened wide as he slid his entire length down her throat. She twirled her tongue around the head of his erection, grazing his entire length with her teeth as his dick thrust further into her mouth. He fucked her face until he blew his load down the back of her throat.

"I love how you love me only the way you can," Rumpel blurted out before he could register what he said.

Gothel's eyes softened as she stared up at him. "Love," she teased.

"I—, yes, love," he admitted to her.

"I love you too," she said unsteadily.

Gothel never planned on giving her heart to anyone. She had always been a heavily guarded woman.

"Are you ready for your next treat," Rumpel teased, his dick already hard for her again.

"Am I ever," she said, nearly drooling.

Rumpel took her legs and threw them over her shoulder, leaving the anal plug inside her asshole. She yelled out as he thrust into her, taking no care to be gentle with her. He had to punish her for being a naughty girl.

"Harder," Gothel breathed as he pumped away.

Rumpelstiltskin gave her everything he had, bringing her to a whole new level of pleasure. The orgasm that she experienced as they spiraled together was the best she had ever experienced. "I think I know exactly how we can solve your hairy situation," Rumpelstiltskin smiled.

Chapter Nine

A Mother's Betrayal

GOTHEL LEFT THE HOTEL with Rumpel, hand in hand. They faced the nightly autumn chill together. Rumpelstilt-

skin wrapped his coat around Gothel as she shivered. They walked into the forest on the outskirts of Sapphire city; it was time to check on Rapunzel. She had to be up to no good.

"I had a daughter once," Rumpelstiltskin's mind wandered as he spoke.

Gothel remained silent. Shock filled her being, and she couldn't find the right words to say to him. She watched as his face twisted and contorted, thinking back on his memories. She didn't dare to snap him out of it for fear of backlash that might occur.

The little bundle of joy that was born in his home was the only life he had ever cared about. Her beautiful golden-brown eyes and dark locks of hair made him fall in love in an instant. He knew from here on out—that this little girl would have him wrapped around her pinky finger. He would do anything for her. He would die for her; he would kill for her. His marriage was forced on him by his parents to raise their station in the community. No one truly wanted to marry an impish-looking man... Their marriage was loveless and cold— to the point of no return. They fought constantly; his wife often threatened to take their daughter and run.

Rumpelstiltskin wouldn't let that happen. One night, as his wife peacefully slept, he held a pillow over her face until she was no longer breathing. He wrapped his baby girl up in blankets and ran off into the night.

No one ever saw him again. Rumpelstiltskin and his daughter led a harsh life. They lived in a rundown shack in the middle of the forest, in a land far from where he was now. Over the years, his daughter grew into a beautiful young woman. Rumpelstiltskin couldn't believe such beauty could have come from him.

The only thing this man loved more than his daughter was the thought of wealth and power. These factors consumed him so much that he and his daughter became estranged. They may have lived together, but life was never so lonely. They often stayed at opposite ends of the beaten shack and barely spoke.

Rumpelstiltskin had a plan. He brought his daughter before the King of the land and promised him something he knew he could never deliver. He pushed his daughter toward the king. "My lord, did you know this child could spin straw into gold," he asked the king.

The king's eyes lit up. "Lies," he spat.

"A lie has never spilled from these lips. This child is special—magical even," He smiled at the king.

"If she proves this to be true, I will marry her. Your family will be one of the wealthiest families in the land. If she fails to deliver your promise, she will die," the king said in a sinister manner.

His daughter's face fell. She knew then and there that she was doomed to die a horrific death.

No matter how estranged they were, fear consumed Rumpel's heart.

"Deal," Rumpel piped up.

Soon, all the wealth and power would be his; nothing and nobody would get in his way. The thought brought him to a state of ecstasy that he had never felt in his life. He had grown up poor, and he was treated like trash by the village around him. Other kids would kick him, punch him, and shove him to the ground. Rumpel was always too small and weak to fight back, so he would lay on the ground enduring the torture from the other kids around him.

"She will be locked in the tower with a spinning wheel and straw until she can produce the gold you have promised. No matter how long it takes," the king smirked.

The King's wife looked at him with disgust. They had been married for so long that it was the only life she ever knew. She thought nothing could break their eternal bond. She thought he was in love with her, but she was wrong. How could he want to be rid of her so badly? Was she really the ugly hag he made her feel like at this moment?

Rumpelstiltskin jumped as a few of the king's guards grabbed his daughter's arms and dragged her off to the tower. He reached after her— but got a glare from the king.

"She is mine now, no matter what her fate might be," his eyes were cold as he spoke.

"Madeline was taken from me, but I vowed to get her back," Rumpelstiltskin finally spoke as he snapped out of his flashback.

"Taken?" Gothel's heart raced as the thought of her and Rapunzel's past ran through her mind. This was a past Rumpel could never discover, or she would lose him.

"I promised someone something I knew she couldn't deliver," he sighed as his shoulders fell. "Wealth and power possessed my mind, and I could think of nothing else. My thoughts should have been on my daughter's safety."

"I'm so sorry, my dear," Gothel caressed his cheek as she spoke.

Before she knew it, Rumpelstiltskin had the same lost look he had on his face. She had lost him to memories again.

Rumpelstiltskin searched to the ends of the earth to find a way to get his daughter back. He realized he had made a grave mistake the moment the guards dragged his baby girl away. The impish man stood in a cave in a distant land. Before him was an old woman. Her hands were in the air, tracing odd symbols into the air. The environment around them changed. Rumpelstiltskin had never truly believed in magic until now.

"Please, wise lady. Help me," he fell to his knees begging.

"Why should I help a stranger like you," the woman hissed.

Rumpelstiltskin wracked his brain for reasons she should help but came up blank. The hag continued to stare at him, waiting for a reply.

"Well..." she sighed.

"My daughter was taken from me due to my own stupidity," the small man stared at his feet as he spoke. Confrontation was never his forte.

"That's not my problem," the witch scoffed at him.

Rumpel's eyes filled with horror as the witch's hands rose into the air again. Only this time, Rumpelstiltskin flew into the air as well.

"Did you really think just coming here was going to solve all of your problems," the witch cackled. "Magic can be a very dangerous force; it all comes at a cost. Magic is all about balance. What I do is always returned in some way. Whether it be a good way or a bad way," the witch explained.

"So, all magic—comes with a price?" Rumpelstiltskin stuttered as he spoke.

"BINGO," the witch yelled as she flung the small man across the cave. "Over my dead body, will I help you with anything at all!" the witch's eyes grew in fear as she spoke.

Rumpelstiltskin crashed into the wall; his breath was stolen from the impact. That didn't stop him from seeing the look on her face when she said this.

"Please," he choked.

"LEAVE," the witch yelled at him. "Leave now with your life, or else."

Rumpel scrambled to his feet and ran out of the cave as fast as his feet would carry him. The darkness swallowed him whole as he ran into the night. Rumpel so fast and so far that he found himself in a dense thicket. He knew he had to find a way to get the witch to help, even if it meant...

Rumpelstiltskin tried to shake the thought from his head, but he would have to force her hand.

"I had to kill for my power, take the life of someone I didn't even know. But I just wanted my daughter back, and I knew with the hag's magic, I could deliver what I promised to the king," he explained.

"You—you've taken a life," Gothel said, a look of stupor on her face.

"Only for the ones I *love*," he said as he caressed his lover's face.

Gothel melted in response to his touch. She gazed into his eyes as he looked back into Her's.

"I found this dagger in a field near the thicket; it was as if it appeared just for me. To fulfill my purpose, to get my daughter back," he said as his face fell. "This dagger was stunning and full of a power I had never felt in my life. As I ran, I felt stronger and stronger. By the time I reached the witch's cave, I felt like I could take on the entire world. The strength I felt was a heady feeling."

Gothel stared at him in wonderment as she spoke. In this moment, she knew she was the luckiest woman alive to have a man like Rumpelstiltskin by her side.

"I ran to the cave, and the witch was asleep. I entered the cave as quietly as I could. As I raised the dagger above the witch's chest, she awoke. I was flung across the cave again, but that didn't stop me. I ran back toward her, knocking her to the ground. She tried to raise her hands again, but I knocked them to the ground. As she struggled beneath me, I raised the dagger into the air and drove it into her still-beating heart," he explained.

"That is—the sexiest thing I have ever heard," Gothel gushed.

"You mean—-you're not scared of me?" he asked.

"Scared? Why—" Gothel trailed off.

"I'm a monster," Rumpel told her. "A cold-blooded monster."

"Not the man I know," Gothel told him as she kissed his forehead. "You are a brave man who would do anything to see the ones he loves happy and healthy."

A smile crossed his face, a smile that Gothel had never seen before. It was a look of gratitude. No one had ever made him feel this way before, and no one had ever felt the same about him, either.

"Anyways," Rumpel continued. "I felt an immense power surge through me, and just the thought of me being with my daughter teleported me to her side," a tear filled his eye. "I was too late; she couldn't deliver what was promised, and she lay cold on the floor. Her eyes were frozen open in fear. From the looks of things, the king had had his way with her before he took her life. This is my deepest regret, having such a thirst for wealth and power," he began to sob.

Gothel held him in her arms, unsure of what to say to him.

"I am so sorry," she whispered to him.

"Found the king shortly after, and I murdered him in cold blood. I Didn't even need magic; the man was a coward. He didn't even fight back as I snapped his neck. His wife screamed in terror, but she was next," he told his love.

"You got your revenge," Gothel trailed off.

"But it's not enough; it'll never be enough. All the money and the power in the world won't bring Madeline back," he wiped a tear from his eye as he spoke.

As he regained his composure, he remembered why he brought up the story that destroyed his life. He needed to help Gothel disempower Rapunzel's hair before she hurt someone or, even worse—killed them.

"We can spin her hair to straw," he chuckled. "It won't be a true straw, but a magical coating to stop her hair from draining the life out of the people around her. You see—I think she had control of her hair when she attacked you. All teens lie, and I believe what she told you was a flat-out lie."

"That little bitch," Gothel's words shocked her more than she thought they would. She had never spoken badly about her daughter, but she was so angered by what she had done—and how she had lied to her own mother.

"You must understand, though, that all magic has its cost," he cautioned his lover.

"I am all in," Gothel replied. "Whatever it takes."

Chapter Ten

Hair Made of Straw

It was late by the time Mother Gothel and Rumpelstiltskin made it back to the tower. Owls could be heard screeching from the uppermost part of the trees in the forest. The wind howled behind them as they stopped at the front wall of the tower, where the window would allow them entrance to the main room. Rumpel turned to his lover when they arrived at the window. She thought that Rapunzel should be asleep by now, making their plan easier to execute.

"How do we climb the tower? You had mentioned boarding up the entrance," he asked his lover.

"It's not rocket science, dear," Gothel replied. "We most certainly won't be asking Rapunzel for help."

She walked over to the side of the tower, where she produced a large ladder she had purchased in town. Rumpel rushed to help her bring the ladder to the wall so they could climb into the tower. She wouldn't risk the wrath of her daughter's hair ever again. Next time, she might crumble to dust if Rapunzel had her way.

"Climb this ladder; I will be right behind you," Gothel whispered to Rumpel.

"You want me to go first," he asked her, surprised.

"You are much quicker than I am; I want you to be in there in case she wakes before anything goes wrong," Gothel explained.

"Anything for you, my queen," he purred at her as he kissed her hand.

Rumpelstiltskin grabbed the first rung of the ladder and began to climb. He was up the ladder before Gothel had time to speak another word. The dark smile that crossed her face could have robbed the moon of its light.

Rumpel looked over the sill of the window when he was inside the tower. He motioned for Gothel to start climbing. Gothel nervously grabbed the rung of the ladder, suddenly fearing something would go gravely wrong. Her heart thumped wildly in her chest as she climbed. She struggled to make it up the ladder, nearly slipping from the oceans of sweat on her palms.

When she made it to the top of the ladder, her foot accidentally knocked into it as she climbed through the window. The ladder went crashing to the ground below, causing Gothel's anxiety to worsen.

"It's okay, I've got you, queen," Rumpelstiltskin reassured her.

Gothel sighed as she melted into Rumpel's arms. Suddenly, she had doubts about tonight's plans being executed properly.

In Rapunzel's Room

Rapunzel's eyes flew open when she heard something come crashing to the ground outside. She found it odd that there was any noise at all. It was always silent in her section of the forest. She found herself blind in the room she had slept in all her life. The little things she knew to maneuver the room without tripping had skipped her mind. Her teeth began to chatter in fear as she rose from her bed. As she swung her legs over the side of her bed, she heard faint whispers from the other room.

Was someone here to hurt her?

Rapunzel lifted herself from her bed, creeping toward her door as quietly as possible. She peeked out the door, but much to her disappointment, her wide eyes caught nobody in sight. Rapunzel knew from the books she had read when she was younger that things would never turn out that easily. She shook in fear as the thought of leaving her room surfaced in her mind. Her eyes darted in each direction up and down the hall. She didn't see anyone, but surely, they would hear her tiptoeing down the hall. Rapunzel pulled the door open slightly further, sticking her head through the crack to see if anyone was coming her way.

In The Main Room

Gothel and Rumpelstiltskin huddled in a corner just out of view of the hallway. Gothel was still on high alert from the ladder that had crashed into the ground. She knew Rapunzel heard it; it was only a matter of time before something went wrong.

Rumpel caressed her face and commanded her attention, turning her face toward his.

"Everything will be okay, beautiful," he told her. "This plan will be executed, even if it's not the exact turnout we expected. Rapunzel's hair will be spun to straw, stopping her from hurting you or anyone else around her ever again."

The witch sighed. "Okay, I guess I can trust you." "You guess," Rumpel looked at her with a coy smile.

"I'm sorry, I am anxious and afraid that this will turn out to be a disaster," her shoulders slumped as she admitted this.

"Do you have absolutely no faith in me," Rumpel asked as he put his hands on his hips.

"No, No, it's not you. It's me who would fuck something up and destroy our entire scheme. My nerves are shot," she whispered to her lover.

Rumpelstiltskin took her hand in hers, planting a light kiss on top of it. Gothel let out a sigh as he did so, allowing herself to calm down and move forward with their plan.

"Everything will be okay; we are in this together. No matter what. I got you, and you got me," he said. "Am I right?"

Gothel nodded at the man before her, unable to form words in her mind to reply to him.

"We will need supplies," he said quietly.

Gothel reached to the shelf behind her and grabbed a small, handheld spinning wheel she and Rapunzel had used when Rapunzel was a child.

"Rapunzel, grab your spinning wheel and come sit down in Mama's lap," Gothel called to her daughter.

"Ooooh, mama, is it time for our favorite story," Rapunzel tilted her head as she asked.

"Yes, baby, it's time for the story of Tom Tit Tot," Gothel chuckled as she pulled Rapunzel into her lap.

Gothel loved listening to Rapunzel clapping in excitement as she brought the book into their laps. She enjoyed the way that Rapunzel snuggled into her bosom as they began the story. The bond between a mother and her daughter was inseparable.

"Tell me everything, Mommy, the whole story this time; I promise

to stay quiet," Rapunzel giggled as she began to twirl her hair in her fingers.

Gothel always loved her little girl's shining gold locks.

"Okay, baby, here comes the story of Tom Tit Tot," Gothel said as she flipped the first page over.

She chuckled as she felt Rapunzel squirm in her lap. She read aloud as she saw Rapunzel spin the little wheel, she had brought home from Sapphire City. Only this time, as she read, she did not notice that her daughter was spinning her golden hair into the wheel.

"Look, mama, my hair is gold," Rapunzel shouted as Gothel finished up the story.

"Oh no, Rapunzel, look at your hair," Gothel said, chuckling as she waved her finger in the air.

"What hair? It's gold now!" Rapunzel shouted as she hopped off her mother's lap and ran around the room.

Gothel chased after her as they giggled; when Rapunzel was in Gothel's arms, they sat together and untangled her blonde hair from the wheel. Both laughed as the chore was finished.

Gothel faked a look of surprise on her face. "Oh my, Rapunzel!

Your hair IS gold. I should be able to fetch a pretty little penny for you on the market," Gothel said as she tickled her little one.

Rapunzel cracked up as she said, "Oh, mama, you wouldn't trade me for the world; that's what you always say, isn't it," Rapunzel's eyes found Gothel's as she pulled her in for a big hug,

"You are right, Rapunzel; I wouldn't trade you for the world," Gothel repeated to her child.

Gothel snapped out of her reverie as Rumpelstiltskin snatched the wheel from her hand.

"Perfect," Rumpel said with a grin. "Thank you," he kissed Gothel softly, tracing patterns on her cheek with his forefinger.

He could feel her start to relax with his gesture.

"I'll go wake Rapunzel," Gothel said, trying to gather her thoughts and carry out their plan effectively.

Rumpelstiltskin nodded as he winked at Gothel. He stood in a corner where he would be undiscovered by anxious eyes. He was unaware of the moon's light, giving away his position. As the moon rose to its position over the window of the tower, so too, did Rapunzel. However, the crashing sound was what woke her that night.

Gothel pushed the door to Rapunzel's door open and was surprised to see that nobody was sleeping in her bed. Much to her surprise, Rapunzel was hidden between her door and the wall. Rapunzel raised a frying pan in the air; fear had stolen her ability to breathe or speak. But her anger was the force that allowed her to act when she watched her mother enter the room.

Before Gothel could look in Rapunzel's direction, a thud could be heard down the hall as Gothel hit the floor.

"And you think I'm up to no good, mother," Rapunzel said as she stepped over her mother's body and out of her bedroom.

When she reached the hall, she noticed a small, impish man standing at the end of it, just before the main room. Her mouth fell open as she looked at him; the moon illuminated his features.

"Tom Tit Tot!" she yelled in amazement.

"No, not quite," she heard from the small man. "Rumpelstiltskin's the name; taming your hair is my game," he said as his head jerked to the side. The evil grin on his face rattled Rapunzel's bones.

Her hair began to fly into the air, trying to capture Rumpel in its grasp. She found her body unable to move as her eyes fixed on the small wheel he was spinning in his hands. "Taming my hair," she asked in confusion.

"Your hair," he said. "This was supposed to go much more smoothly, but the ladder must have startled you awake."

"My hair does not need" — Rapunzel froze as her dark hair began to spin into the wheel, as if by magic.

"Shush, little one, it will all be over soon," Rumpel said maliciously.

Her body began to weaken as the hair entered the wheel. Rapunzel found herself dizzy and full of anxiety as she watched her hair spin into the wheel in horror. She felt like a giant, wet noodle. Somehow, Rumpelstiltskin had stolen her strength, too.

"Round and round the deadly hair spins; when it's complete, it's Rumpel who wins," he cackled.

Once her hair was completely wound into the wheel, Rumpelstiltskin snapped his fingers. The wheel vanished, leaving behind a room full of straw that was once Rapunzel's hair.

Rapunzel fell to the ground as she watched her black locks turn to what could only be described as straw. She held her hair in her hands, and tears streamed down her face, knowing that her beauty was gone, that her power was no more. The straw she had for hair had looked as if it would break into pieces when it hit the ground. She thought her hair was swift enough, but it wasn't. It was now confined to a permanent straw prison, and the beast had swallowed the key.

"My hair," she cried. "What have you done," she tried to compel her hair to move, but all it did was lay lifeless on the ground.

"All you need to know is I've done my part, and no one is here to fix the pieces of your broken heart," he said as he wandered toward her bedroom.

"You will regret this," Rapunzel threatened.

"Pah, you have no ammo to back your threat; good luck, deary," he cackled as he slinked even closer to the room where Gothel lay on the floor.

By the time he made it to the bedroom, Gothel was stirring awake, rubbing her head.

Rapunzel ran for her room, but by the time she peered inside, all she caught was a glimpse of Rumpelstilskin and her mother into thin air.

Chapter Eleven

Magics Toll

Gothel felt a whirr as she was transported back to the safety of their hotel room. She had no idea what happened; all she knew was that she had a splitting headache. She looked over at Rumpelstiltskin, and the sinister smile that stretched across his face told her everything she needed to know.

"The war is not over, but we have won this battle," he winked at Gothel as he planted a soft kiss on her forehead.

"You, did it? Her hair—," Gothel trailed off as she rubbed her tender head.

"Her long black locks are now brittle straw," he smiled at his lover.

Gothel slumped for a second. She was worn down by the blow she took to her head.

She placed her hand on her head. "Did Rapunzel do this to me," she asked.

"With a frying pan," Rumpel admitted as he looked at the ground.

"Oh," she said, feeling a little hurt that her own daughter attacked her. "I am so tired."

"You cannot sleep yet; I need to keep an eye on you for a while," Rumpelstiltskin explained as he caressed her hand. "You might have a serious concussion; you were knocked out for a while back at the tower."

"I—I don't remember anything," Gothel told him.

"Let's play a game," he told her charmingly.

"A game," she asked, her head spinning.

"It will be fun, promise," he told her.

"What game do you propose we play," Gothel asked him.

Rumpelstiltskin tapped his finger to his chin, contemplating how to entertain Gothel to keep her awake.

"Truth or dare," Rumpel asked Gothel, catching her off guard.

"Uhm, Truth," Gothel said, thinking she was safe.

"Tell me something about you that nobody knows," Rumpel said with a grin.

Gothel froze. The first thing that crossed her mind was the last thing she ever wanted her lover to find out. She pondered for a moment before deciding on what she was going to reveal.

"Before you, I hadn't been with another man in over 20 years," she admitted to him.

He nodded his head, lost in thought.

"That was not the first thing that popped into your mind. You have something you are afraid to share with me, and I want to know what it is," he sneered. "I saw the look in your eyes when I first asked you, and it piqued my interest. Do not lie to me, or I will know."

"I—I um," she stammered.

"I'm waiting," he said impatiently.

He already knew something was up between her and Rapunzel. There was no way that beautiful child was hers. There was something amiss. No mother would ever want to break their child's spirit in the way that she did.

"Rapunzel is not my child," she sighed as her shoulders slumped.

"There is still something you are not telling me. Out with it," Rumpel commanded.

"Alright, Alright," she cried. "I'm sorry. Rapunzel was born to a poor family close to my home. I caught them stealing food from me during hard times, and I took their child as payment for their wrongdoing."

Rumpelstiltskin's rage was palpable. She could see the veins ready to burst on his forehead. His fists were balled tightly, and he didn't blink once. She shuffled backward out of fear of being struck by the anger-stricken man in front of her.

"You WHAT," he growled. "You took a child from their parents before they even got a chance to know her. "That right there is a cold-blooded monster," he pointed at her as he spoke. "I can't believe a human could be so cruel. I would give anything to have my Madeline back, as I am sure Rapunzel's parents are missing her."

Gothel remained silent. She knew the end of their shortlived relationship was looming. She had wished he didn't have to find out this way; she would have preferred it if he had never found out at all.

"Oh, I won't strike you," he told her. "But I will never lay eyes or hands on you again. Your shit choices will destroy your life; I can promise you this," he ground his teeth as he walked out of the room and slammed the door behind him.

Gothel was left to sob on her own. The rose petals and candles that had surrounded the room had since vanished, leaving behind a heatless flame of the relationship they could have had. Now, she had no one, and she had nowhere to go. *And it was all her own fault.*

Back at the Tower

Rapunzel sat for hours stroking the pieces of straw that used to be her best attribute. Her songs at the window would be fruitless once the man saw the straw she had for hair. The new day had broken, and the circles under her eyes told the nightmarish tales of the misdeeds that had been brought upon her by her own mother. She stroked her hair, taking care not to catch one of the straw splinters under her skin.

Rapunzel braided the straw, fearing it would break as she did so. Much to her surprise, her hair was still as resilient as it had been when it was black; it was just dull and lifeless. Rapunzel roamed about the tower, trying to figure out a way to get her hair back.

Something in her told her to search through Gothel's room. There had to be a reason Gothel had always forbidden her from going in there, and until now, it didn't click.

She had deep-seated secrets she wasn't planning on sharing, ever.

Rapunzel tiptoed into her mother's room, hoping to find spells or something that might undo the magic that Rumpelstiltskin had used to destroy her hair. She looked under the bed, only to find her mother's armory of sex toys, some she had never seen before.

She rose from her search under the bed, and her eyes shifted over to the night table beside her mother's bed. The drawer

was left slightly ajar, and she noticed a small black book inside. Rapunzel wrapped her hands around the small leather book and removed it from the drawer. When she did, she expected to find spells. But what Rapunzel found was much different than a spell.

September 14th,

Today, I caught people across the field stealing food from me. I cannot believe the audacity of these people! But I will let it slide this one time... they look like they are struggling.

October 2nd,

They have been stealing from me for over a month now; their faces no longer show guilt. Have they no shame in committing a crime? I need to find a way to make them pay... I will find the perfect way... I need time to think.

October 18th,

The wife of the couple who has been stealing from me seems to be with-child. I know the perfect retribution for their sins. The child will be mine. They will never see me or that child ever again.

October 28th,

I can hear the pains of labor in the mother's screams from across the field. I know the baby will be here soon. And soon, I will have a small child to call my own. I hope it's a girl; I have always wanted a girl. I have to wait for the perfect moment and swoop in to take my prize..

A tear dropped onto the page as Rapunzel kept reading. The eyes she kept seeing popped into her head. Gothel *wasn't* her biological mother, as she had always thought. She was a monster who stole a couple's baby right from their home.

All the young woman could see now was red. She had to get back at Gothel for robbing her of the right to grow up with her true family. Revenge was heavy on her mind throughout the day. In order to get revenge on Gothel, she had to find a way to reverse the spell.

Rumpelstiltskin.

The thought of him came to her mind just as she began to lose hope. She thought of the story of Tom Tit Tot from when she was a child. He bore a striking resemblance to the impish man from the story. She wondered if his magic worked the same way.

Surely, his name wouldn't give her power over him; he had told her his name. But there had to be another way to get him here in front of her. Rapunzel grabbed a handheld mirror from her mother's bathroom.

"Rumpelstiltskin, Rumpelstiltskin, trouble is thou name. Rumpelstiltskin, magic is thou game," she whispered as she peered into the mirror.

She found herself holding the mirror up to show her the area surrounding her. She nearly jumped off the bed when she saw Rumpelstiltskin standing behind her.

"Hello, Child," he greeted the straw-haired girl.

"Rumpelstiltskin," Rapunzel nodded to him.

"It seems we started off on the wrong foot," he said, regretting his words.

"Wrong foot, huh," she peered back at him begrudgingly.

"My child, I had no idea that Gothel was such a monster," he sighed. "She made you out to be the monster."

"I suppose that's why she has locked me away my whole life— because I am a monster? I have only been outside of these walls once, in the dark and over by the tree out front. I have no idea what the world is like because she told me it was a dangerous place," she snapped.

"You are no monster, child. I see that now," Rumpel told her soothingly.

Rapunzel stomped her foot on the ground in frustration. She just wanted this nightmare to be over.

"If I am no monster, then fix my hair!" she screamed at him.

"Ah, but this isn't a spell that I can undo, but one that can only be broken by the imbued," he told her.

"Oh yeah, and how do you expect me to do that," she asked him.

As she turned around to look at him, he vanished. She screamed in frustration, unsure of how to break the spell. Her immediate thoughts were ones of leaving the tower. She knew Gothel kept tools around the tower somewhere, so she

wandered off in search of them.

She was in luck when she found a large sledgehammer in an unused closet outside of Gothel's room. Rapunzel dragged the sledgehammer behind her and down the stairs of the tower.

She was suddenly brought back to the first time she had snuck away from the tower.

She tiptoed down the stairs and pushed the door open. The grass beneath her tickled her bare toes as she shuffled forward. It was dark outside, and the world looked different from the ground. She had always had a window view of the world when she was trapped in the tower.

Anxiety filled her mind as she listened to the noises of the night. When she couldn't take it any longer, she ran back into the tower, tracking the grass and mud up the stairs that she had been yelled at about later. She locked herself in her room that evening as she listened to her mother hammer away at the door, sealing it shut—so she could never escape again.

Rapunzel lifted the sledgehammer but dropped it right away. It was a weight she wasn't used to. She wasn't going to give up, though; she would escape the tower if it were the last thing she did. Rapunzel closed her eyes and gathered her strength. This was something she knew she could do.

The young straw-haired woman raised the sledgehammer in the air once more. She swung it at the door with the strength she didn't know she had. She could see the wood breaking apart from her efforts. It took quite a few more swings before the boarded-up doors were broken open. She smelled freedom as the fresh air caressed her cheeks.

Rapunzel took a deep breath as she took her first step outside.

Freedom.

Chapter Thirteen

The Family Lineage

Rays of sunshine peaked through Rapunzel's curtains early the next morning. Her thoughts wandered to

Flynn Rider, the irresistible man she met the evening before. She wondered what time he was going to come for her – the bigger question was *how he was going to find her*. It seemed as if not many knew about the tower deep in the woods.

Rapunzel reached her hand up to scratch her itchy scalp. She groaned as she was reminded that her hair was now made of straw. She loathed Rumpelstiltskin for causing her so much heartache. The sweat-laden pajamas led her to believe she had had a nightmare the night before. This has been a frequent thing lately.

She stood alone in a dark room. The silence was deafening and seemed to swallow her whole. The only thing she could hear was the rustling of her straw hair. She searched for a way to free herself from the room, but there seemed to be no windows or doors. Rapunzel screamed for help, but no one would come to her aid.

"You're unworthy," she kept hearing over and over. "No one will ever want you with hair made of straw," Rapunzel slumped as she heard this.

At first, Rapunzel fought back, knowing she was worthy of love. After hearing the voice enough, though, she started to believe the venom that was being spewed at her.

"Love will never be yours," it screamed at her. "You're doomed to an eternity of loneliness."

Rapunzel fell to the ground, crying out in pain.

Just when she thought it couldn't get any worse, she felt her straw hair begin to wrap around her body. It began to squeeze her body, crushing her rib cage. She started to scream out in pain, but her hair wrapped around her mouth, silencing her. She wriggled and struggled, trying to break free, until she vanished...never to be seen again.

Rapunzel trembled as she remembered her dream. She had to find a way to force it out of her mind before she succumbed to a panic attack. The growls in her stomach brought her into the present. Breakfast. She knew eating a hardy meal was a good way to ground herself and quell the anxiety rising inside of her.

She shuffled her feet until she reached the kitchen. Looking in the fridge, it seemed the only sustenance in the house was eggs and fruit. Rapunzel swayed her hips as she hummed. She spun around, bringing eggs to the bowl one by one and cracking them. Scrambled eggs were always her favorite.

She beat the eggs with a fork, carefully pouring them into the heated pan on the stove. As the eggs cooked on the stove, she went to the fridge and grabbed the grapes and strawberries.

She swiftly sliced them up, mixing them in a bowl.

When she got back to her scrambled eggs, they were more of an omelet. She lifted the omelet from the pan, sliding it onto her plate. When her food was all prepared, she brought her bowl, plate, and utensils into the main room, where she plopped in the giant bean bag chair.

Rapunzel took her time, mindfully eating the food. Her stomach was satiated by the time she finished. She was content until the memories of her "mother" came flooding into her mind. She always loved story time as a child. Especially when she got to spin her wheel listening to the story of Tom tit tot, she *hated this story now. It reminded her of the crazy straw hair that now inhabited her head.*

Rapunzel was pulled from her reverie when she heard a whistle from outside of the window. She peeked over the windowsill to see Ryder's beautiful black curls cascading down to his shoulders. He wore a tight black shirt and jeans. His chest was muscular, and he stood proud. He was looking around the field as he spoke.

"Rapunzel," he shouted. "Are you there?"

Rapunzel couldn't believe he had found her. He really was good at his job.

"I'm here, Flynn," she called down to him. "The door is around back, well... the lack of."

Flynn shot her a puzzled look as he began to step around the side of the tower. Within seconds, he was at her side.

"Howdy, milady," he greeted her.

"Well, hello to you too, kind sir," she curtsied.

He chuckled. The look in her eyes made him nervous. A woman with straw hair really was not his type. He felt terrible at the thought of it, but it was just the truth.

"I can smell the old witch strongly here," he said, his nose turned up in the air.

"She was just here last night," Rapunzel told him. "She tried to take something from me, but I stopped her. I tripped her as she went down the stairs and went to hide the book, but when

I came back, she was gone." "What did she try to take," he asked.

"Well, I found this small leather-bound book in a run-down shop. When I opened it, the pages began to glow. I hoped it had the answers I was looking for to reverse this—mess," she said with a disgruntled look on her face.

"Sounds like a grimoire, a powerful one at that," Rider said, tapping his chin.

"A *Grimoire*," Rapunzel asked.

"A magical spell book, although most don't glow like the one you found," Flynn explained.

He brushed his curly black hair back with his fingers, removing the curls from his face. Rapunzel was nearly drooling when he looked up at her. She tried to hide it, but she failed miserably.

"You're not really my type, ya know," Flynn said reluctantly.

"Oh..." Rapunzel said, her heart shattering. "I guess I saw that coming."

"Saw what was coming?" Flynn asked, his head tilted to the side.

"It's nothing," she sighed, trying to divert the topic.

The look on her face caused Flynn to regret his words. He could see all over her face that she was struggling with insecurities and woes.

"I'm sorry, I shouldn't have been so harsh," he said. "I shoulda left it alone."

Rapunzel's mind wandered to her nightmares. Was her intuition trying to tell her something? Or were her insecurities shadowing her mind? She shook the thoughts from her mind, trying to focus on the events that were about to unfold.

"Let me see that book of yours," Rider said.

"Oh, um...okay," Rapunzel wandered off and grabbed the book from its hiding place. "Here you go."

Flynn took the book from her hands, turning it over in his own. He inspected the entire outer cover before opening the book. When he opened the book, it remained lifeless.

"It's empty," he said.

"Is not," Rapunzel argued.

"Is too," Flynn fought back.

"Let me see it," Rapunzel snatched the book from his hands.

When she thumbed through the grimoire, words began to appear on the pages. She was stunned at the power she felt emanating from the book's pages.

"See, look here," she pointed at the page the book stopped on.

"A blank page," Flynn sighed. "You sure you're not some sorta psycho or something?"

Rapunzel's hands flew to her hips as she glared at him.

"No, I'm perfectly sane. Thank you very much," she stuck her tongue out at him as she spoke.

Rapunzel began to read the words she saw on the front page of the grimoire.

"Wisdom of the Old Ones," she read.

"Stop making shit up, Rapunzel. You found a journal. That's all it is," he chastised her.

"What I am reading is here, I swear," she told him.

"Passed down along the lineage of the Ashenbrook witches," Rapunzel continued.

"Ashenbrook," Flynn repeated. "That is a powerful line of witches."

"This ancient text is hidden from prying eyes. Only witches with the Ashenbrook blood can see the spells contained in this grimoire."

"You're a witch," Flynn said, his mouth falling open in shock.

"I'm nothing like Gothel," Rapunzel yelled, throwing the book across the room.

"No—you don't understand," he explained. "Not all witches practice baneful magic."

"Baneful," Rapunzel repeated.

"Evil, wrong, dark, the kind that is meant to inflict harm on others," he told her.

"Oooh, I see," Rapunzel chirped.

Rapunzel walked across the room and picked up the grimoire. She opened the book, and the pages started to turn on their own. When it finally stopped, it rested on a peculiar page.

"The Chosen Child" – Rapunzel read.

"One day, a child will be born with special hair. This can restore youth when the child is content or will cause people to rapidly age and kill them when the child is upset and feels betrayed. When the child is content, her hair will be a golden blonde; when betrayed, it will turn black as night," Rapunzel gasped.

"They're talking about me," she said, stumbling over her words.

"But your hair is *straw*," Rider reminded her.

"Rumpelstiltskin cursed me," she jabbed him in the ribs with her elbow.

"Ouch, what was that for," Flynn growled.

"For being a jerk," Rapunzel scorned him.

Rapunzel continued reading and discovered that she was and would be the most powerful witch of her lineage. This grimoire skipped a generation and was lost for years. It was supposed to be passed down to Eve, who was supposed to raise her child and teach her the ways of the Ashenbrook witches.

"Eve," Rapunzel breathed. "So Gothel was never my true mother like her journal says. I didn't want to believe it, but this is confirmation of the monster she truly is." Flynn nodded in response.

"But how do I fix my hair," Rapunzel whined.

"Maybe torturing Gothel will bring us the answers we need," Flynn interjected.

"This wasn't her curse; she had no idea how to reverse it. Even if she was the one who wanted this," Rapunzel explained. "Rumpelstiltskin would be the one to torture, but good luck getting him in the same place for long enough to torture him."

Rapunzel's mind drifted to a fading memory of deep green eyes.

"My mother," she said. "She had green eyes." "How do you know that," Flynn asked her.

"I remember looking into them as a baby," she answered.

"Impossible," Flynn told her.

"Apparently not, not for a witch," she scowled.

Rapunzel looked back down at the book.

"A curse on this hair could spell disaster; this is something that is very hard to fix."

"Great," Rapunzel sighed. "Disaster, just what I wanted.

"Let's go for drinks," Flynn said, trying to lighten the mood. "I've never drank," Rapunzel said sheepishly.

"Well, I'd love to pop your sober cherry then," he said with a smirk.

Flynn grabbed his new friend by the hand and guided her down the tower's steps. He pushed the blanket of a door back, and the brisk autumn air chilled them.

"Maybe a jacket is in order," Rapunzel said, stepping backward.

"Wai—," Flynn started.

Before he could get the word out, Rapunzel was up the stairs. She disappeared from view and came back with a black fur coat.

"It was Gothel's, but it's mine now," she laughed as she pulled her straw hair away from her face.

"Are you ready now, *Princess,*" Flynn teased.

"Lose the attitude, fool," she growled.

Flynn stepped back, afraid to anger her.

"Oh, my hair won't hurt you; it's just lifeless straw," she grumbled. "But if you keep it up, you will catch these hands." Rider nearly fell to the ground laughing.

"Don't you worry; I am not worried about catching those little hands of yours," he scoffed. "Now let's go; we can plot revenge over a drink."

"Only if you're paying," Rapunzel teased.

"What kind of gentleman would I be if I didn't pay," he chuckled.

"You're no gentleman at all," she poked at him.

"I'm not buying with that attitude," he laughed.

The two of them walked down the path toward the city. Rapunzel was nervous about drinking for the first time with a man who was basically a stranger. She had never let loose before, but this was her chance. She had a feeling today would be a fun-filled day.

Chapter Fourteen

Day Drinking

Flynn and Rapunzel arrived at the pub a little after noon. He pushed the door open, and Rapunzel's senses were filled with the smell of fried food and alcohol.

"Do you think we could grab a bite to eat, too?" Rapunzel asked.

"No drinking on an empty stomach. That's rule number one. Doing so would lead to disaster."

Rapunzel stepped inside, followed by Flynn. Flynn grabbed her hand and led her to a spot at the bar. He patted the barstool next to him, motioning for Rapunzel to sit down. Rapunzel plopped on the stool, giggling as the bartender eyed her up and down.

"Maybe he is staring at your straw hair," Rider teased.

"Nah, that was more of a fuck me look," Rapunzel whispered as she winked at Flynn.

The two of them giggled in tandem until the waiter came to the bar.

"What'll you have today, my good people," the tall, thin waiter asked.

"Two orders of cheese fries and two burgers all the way," Flynn said proudly. "A martini for the lady and a shiner for me."

"Coming right up," the waiter said as he jotted the order down on his pad.

The waiter whisked away after handing the drink ticket to the bartender. As fast as the slip was handed to him, the two drinks were slid down the bar to the waiting customers. Rapunzel went to take a sip, but she was stopped by Flynn.

"Remember what I told you," He warned her. "It will be a miserable day if you start drinking on an empty stomach."

"Yeah, yeah," she said, placing the dainty glass on the bar.

"So, about that witch, you live with," Flynn poked at her.

"What are we going to do about her?"

"I haven't fully decided yet. But first, we really need to fix my hair. I feel like that is the only thing powerful enough to take her down. All other magic is a moot point if she is as strong as you say she is," Rapunzel said in a hushed tone.

"You might just be right; we need a plan of action. I'm guessing—" he started, but the food arrived sooner than he expected.

Rapunzel picked up a cheese-covered fry and took a bite.

"This is delicious," she said with her mouth full of food. "I've never had cheese fries before."

"Damn, Rapunzel, have you no decency," Flynn asked.

"What—" Rapunzel said as a piece of fry fell out of her mouth.

"Try chewing your food with your mouth closed and swallowing before you speak," Flynn said with his face scrunched up.

"Sorry," Rapunzel said. "I honestly don't know how to act in public settings."

"I can tell," Rider teased.

Rapunzel ate a few more fries before she started to eat her burger. Flynn watched her eat as he giggled. The contents of the burger spilled onto the plate. Rapunzel then picked up the martini that she had almost forgotten about.

She smelled the drink and scrunched her nose.

"That is one potent scent," she said with a twisted face.

Flynn looked at her in amusement. "Take a sip," he told her.

Rapunzel put the glass to her lips and sipped the martini. Her eyes grew wide as her face scrunched in disgust. She swallowed the alcohol in her mouth before speaking.

"That's disgusting," she said as she shivered in repugnance.

"But it makes you feel so good," Flynn said as he took a big swig of beer.

Rapunzel held her nose and gulped the martini down. The burning feeling in her throat was a new sensation to her.

"It burns," she told Rider.

"It's supposed to," he said. "Would you like to try something a little more—fruity," he asked.

"Yeah, I think that would be a good idea," she admitted.

Flynn flagged down the waiter and ordered another drink for Rapunzel.

"Give me your best peach schnapps; make it sweet on the rocks, please," he told the man at the counter.

"Yessir," the bartender nodded at him.

"You're going to love this," Flynn smiled at her.

"I'll believe that once I taste it," she said, shuttering at the thought of the martini.

Flynn laughed and continued to eat. Rapunzel ate a few more fries and finished her burger.

A large glass was placed in front of her. She inspected the entire glass before she gave it a whiff and took a sip. Her face lit up after she swallowed her first swig.

"This is something I could drink every day," she told Flynn.

"Woah, Woah there, my little alcoholic," Flynn teased.

"About my straw hair," Rapunzel said sheepishly. "What were you saying earlier?"

"I was thinking the answers to your hairy situation could be in that family grimoire you found," he said as he swallowed the last bite of his burger.

"You might be right," Rapunzel gulped her drink down.

"You are going to feel that very soon," he said.

"You're damn right I am," Rapunzel slurred.

The music playing in the background had Rapunzel fired up.

"Hey, you wanna dance, Flynn," she asked him, grabbing his hand and ripping him away from the bar.

"Dancing could be fun," he said.

Rapunzel found the dance floor beside the bar. She began to sway her hips and move her arms. Flynn danced beside her, giggling as he watched her dance.

"Nice moves, straw head," he teased.

"You're not so bad yourself, ya filthy animal," Rapunzel replied.

Rapunzel swayed as she danced, and Flynn barely caught her as she fell.

"I think it's time to leave," Rider told her.

Rapunzel cuddled up to him as he held her.

"At least you don't stink," she giggled.

"Um, thanks," he didn't know how to respond to her comment.

Rider placed money on the table before carrying Rapunzel out of the pub. Rapunzel was wasted, and he knew she wouldn't be walking home. He wasn't going to make it through the woods to the tower with her in his arms.

"Back to the hotel we go," he said, getting a better grip on her. "Okay, handsome," Rapunzel said as she started to doze off.

Flynn cradled her in her arms as he carried her, taking care not to drop her on the ground. His arms grew tired as he walked the few city blocks to the hotel. He may have been strong, but he had never carried another human this far before. The two arrived at the door to the hotel, and Flynn pushed it open with his hip.

"Your room is ready for you, sir," the woman at the concierge told him.

"Thank you kindly," Flynn winked at her.

He watched the lady swoon. He chuckled as he hit the button for the elevator. Their floor was at the top of the building, and his arms were killing him. Though he was committed to taking care of Rapunzel, he was the one who introduced her to the drinking world after all.

Flynn stumbled out of the elevator when they reached the top floor. He was starting to feel the effects of the beer.

"Odd timing, but I'll take it," he murmured to himself.

He struggled to bring the keycard to the sensor with Rapunzel in his arms. He was relieved when the door opened, and he could put her in the bed. Rapunzel curled into a ball the minute she hit the bed.

Flynn decided it was a good time for a shower. He was feeling woozy from the beer, and was worn out from carrying a fullgrown woman to the hotel room from the pub. He closed the bathroom door behind him as he stepped inside. He stripped his clothes and placed them on the toilet before stepping into the steaming hot shower.

The water felt like heaven on his skin as it rinsed away the toils of the day. He found himself thinking of Rapunzel as he showered. Feelings were stirring inside of him that he never planned on having. He could never tell Rapunzel; it would destroy the friendship they were building.

She did think he was hot, though.

Flynn sighed as his dick started to harden. He closed his eyes, imagining the landscapes of Rapunzel's body. Her delicious curves made him want her even more. He grabbed his dick and started to stroke it. The perfect pressure he applied as he jerked made an orgasm build quicker than usual. He finished up and washed himself off.

When he stepped out of the shower, he heard Rapunzel stirring. He wrapped the towel around his waist and left the bathroom to check on her. A puff of steam wafted out of the bathroom as he went. He looked in Rapunzel's direction. She

was sitting up in bed when he reached the bedside table.

"Well, hello there, Ryder," she said, still drunk.

"Hi yourself," he said to her.

"What's that tone I hear in your voice," she asked him. He panicked, "What tone? Go back to sleep. You're drunk." At that, he rushed back into the bathroom to get dressed.

"The Fuck me tone," she yelled after him as she fell over on the bed.

Flynn put his clothes on and brushed his teeth with the supplies the hotel left in the bathroom. He thought about what Rapunzel said, and although she was right—he would never admit it.

When he was finished, he walked out of the bathroom and sat next to Rapunzel in the bed.

"How're you feeling?" he asked her.

"Uhm," she groaned. "Like I'm going to—"

With that, she jumped out of bed and nearly fell, running to the bathroom. Vomit spewed from her mouth into the toilet before she could even shut the door. Flynn walked in and held her hair back so she wouldn't soak it in the contents of her stomach.

Could you even wash straw?

She stood when she was done vomiting.

"Aww," she said as she swayed. "You care about me."
"That's what friends are for," Flynn said, taking her hand.

"Or maybe something more," she said as she wobbled toward the bed, holding onto Rider.

Rapunzel wrapped herself in blankets as she snuggled up in the bed. Flynn lay next to her; worn out from the adventures they had had that day. For a while, they stared into each other's eyes, searching for something to say. Before either of them got a word out, they fell asleep.

Rapunzel's eyes fluttered open early in the morning. She sighed as she watched Flynn sleeping next to her. She wanted to reach out and touch him, but his words haunted her.

"You're really not my type, you know,"

These words mixed with the feelings of unworthiness that shadowed her dreams. Rapunzel was lost in a storm of volatile thoughts and emotions. She bit her lip, trying not to cry, and saw Flynn stretch. His eyes darted open, and he searched the room. It looked as if he sensed something he wasn't saying.

Rapunzel rose from the bed and headed to the bathroom. While in there, she washed her face and brushed her teeth.

When she stepped out of the bathroom, Flynn grabbed her hand.

"We have to go," he said in a hushed voice.

"Wha—" Flynn put his finger to her lip to hush her before she could finish speaking.

"Shh, I smell dirty magic," he explained. "We need to sneak out of this place without being seen. I fear for your safety," he told her.

Rapunzel and Flynn left the room, treading lightly as they went. As they reached the front corridor, Rider pulled her behind a wall. He peeked around the corner and turned to Rapunzel.

"Stay here," he said. "I will go investigate."

When Flynn returned, the color of his face had drained.

"Run," he said.

The two of them ran as fast as they could out of the hotel. They ran into the tree line and back toward the tower. They felt something chasing them, but they didn't dare look back.

When they made it to the tower, the environment around them calmed. Both of them sighed in relief as they leaned on the tower wall for support.

"I need to pee," Rapunzel said as she shuttered from the cold breeze.

She ran through the blanket to the tower and up the stairs.

Flynn followed close behind before she heard a voice.

"It's empty," Gothel gasped.

She threw the white leatherbound book across the room. Rapunzel peeked around the corner and watched as her mother disappeared.

"She really *is* a witch," Rapunzel said in a stupor.

"If that's any confirmation for you," Flynn started. "She is most definitely not of your blood."

Chapter Fifteen

Secrets of the Ashenbrook

Rapunzel ran for the bathroom when she saw the coast was clear. She couldn't believe Gothel had tried to steal her family's grimoire. *Again*. When she stepped out of the bathroom, she noticed Flynn looking around the tower.

"This is a nice place you got here," he mentioned.

"It's not so bad when you're not trapped in it your entire life," she said sarcastically.

"I can't imagine living a life confined to a tower; I'm glad you finally broke free," he uttered.

"Me too—" Rapunzel trailed off.

She stared down the hall at the impish man standing at the end. When she looked over to Rider, she noticed the hair on his body standing on end.

"I smell an impish man," Ryder told Rapunzel.

He looked down the hall and was staring into the eyes of the monster he had been searching for most of his adult life. "Rumpelstiltskin," Flynn growled, cracking his knuckles. "Flynn Rider," Rumpel said nervously. "I come in peace." "You will leave in pieces," Flynn said darkly.

"No—I've come to help," Rumpelstiltskin pleaded.

"Haven't you caused enough pain," Rapunzel screeched.

"I—I, how many times do I have to apologize," Rumpelstiltskin fell to his knees, desperate to escape with his life.

Rumpelstiltskin was unaware that his magic was neutralized once Flynn looked into his eyes. He repeatedly tried to teleport himself out of the tower, but his efforts were futile. He panicked and pulled a dagger from his pocket, pointing it at Flynn.

"Don't come near me, or I'll have no choice," he screamed, as he shuddered in fear.

"You won't be going anywhere, Rumple-foreskin," Rider scoffed.

Rapunzel stifled a laugh as she stared down the hall at the beast who spun her hair into straw.

"How do we fix her hair?" Flynn called to him.

"I—It's very complex," Rumpelstiltskin told him. "It has nothing to do with me and everything to do with the girl standing next to you."

"Thanks for the cryptic response, asshole," Rapunzel shouted. Flynn charged down the hall and grabbed Rumpelstiltskin. He hit the dagger out of his hand, and it hit the floor in front of them. He twisted his arms behind his back and walked him up the hall to the main room. He forced him to the ground, grabbing a blanket to tie his arms up.

Rumpel struggled to break free, but the binding was too tight. Rapunzel grabbed the white leather bound grimoire from the spot on the floor where it landed when Gothel threw it. When she lifted the book off the floor, Rumpelstiltskin's eyes widened in wonderment.

"The Ashenbrook grimoire," he gasped.

"How do you know about this," Rapunzel asked.

"Know about it? It's a legend in the magical world," he explained. "Few have laid their eyes on it; it is rumored that only those who are descended from the Ashenbrook bloodline can see the contents of the book."

"You're right," Rapunzel said matter-of-factly.

"Y-you can see the words in the book," Rumpel stuttered.

"Clear as day," Rapunzel responded proudly.

Rumpelstiltskin was speechless. Deep down, he was a bit terrified. With the magic already coursing through her veins and the knowledge in that book—she'd be the most powerful magical creature in all the land. He would have to try his best to befriend her and get on her good side. The last thing he wanted to do was die.

"The answers you seek are in that book," he said. "You must ask the book to show it to you; it is something it doesn't reveal to just anyone."

"Go on," Rider said.

"Pulling off magic of that magnitude won't be easy," he shook his head as he spoke. "Many fail to find the tools needed to cast

the spell. Not everything is a physical ingredient."
"And," Rapunzel said.

"I don't know the specifics; what I have heard is hearsay," Rumpelstiltskin said.

"So, what you're saying is you're feeding me a line of bullshit," Rider growled as he ripped Rumpel's head back by his hair.

"No—No, I swear, I am telling you the truth," Rumpel said in a strained voice. "There is much to do, and she will have to forego it alone."

Rapunzel sighed. She enjoyed having Flynn Rider by her side, but she would do anything to restore her hair back to what it was. She had much to learn from the grimoire once she did. As she ruminated over the magic contained in the book, one thing kept coming to mind.

"Kill Gothel," she heard it clear in her mind, like the voices in her dreams. "Your hair."

Rapunzel shook her head, trying to make the voices stop.

The two men in the room looked at her as if she were crazy. "What was that about," Flynn asked her.

"The voice," she said. "You didn't hear it?"

"There was no voice deary. What are you talking about," Rumpelstiltskin inquired.

"It was as if someone was standing next to me," she said.

Rapunzel lifted the grimoire to her ear. She heard quiet whispers coming from the pages. At this point, she knew her ancestors were trying to get in contact with her. She was amazed at the power the book held. Rapunzel was still in disbelief that she descended from a line of powerful witches. *It did explain her magical hair, though.*

"Ashenbrook ancestors," Rapunzel started. "How do I spin the straw from my hair?"

The pages started to flip as Rapunzel held the book. The whispers grew louder, but she couldn't make out the words. Finally, the book fell open to a specific page. Flynn stared at the book as it started to glow. The glow from the book filled the entire room, creating a chilling feeling for all sitting around it.

"I can see the glow," he said. "Amazing."

"Now you know I'm not some sort of psycho or something," she rolled her eyes at him.

Rider chuckled, remembering what he had asked her earlier that day.

Rapunzel stared at the pages as words started to appear. The words appearing made it seem as though the grimoire was talking to her.

There is much to be done to restore your hair to its natural state. The spell cast on you is intricate magic that the caster cannot undo. This spell can only be broken by the receiver of the curse. There are many ingredients that are needed that you will have to search far and wide for. The hardest thing to find is your self-worth. Rapunzel, you are the only one with this hair and the only one who can break this magic. Finding the other ingredients is more of a test of your will, but discovering your self-worth is the most important part. Ignore the voices that color your thoughts with negativity. You are worthy of the greatest things in this world, including love. It may seem hard to believe, but you will come to know this in time.

Rapunzel watched as the words on the page disappeared. She was grateful for the advice the book gave, but she was still at a loss for the other things she needed to restore her hair to its natural state. She continued to stare at the book. Moments later, more words began to appear on the pages.

Oh yeah, you might need to know what to look for to spin your straw back into hair. Haha. First, you will need to find a piece of Moldavite, this is a powerful crystal that can be costly in price. The next thing you will need to find is a flower by the name of "tears of the moon," this is one of the most important ingredients. Pixie dust is also on the list, along with the blood of the caster.

Rapunzel's eyes darted over to Rumpel as she read this. She heard an audible gulp come from his throat. He didn't know why she was looking at him like that, but he knew it couldn't be good. Rapunzel looked back down at the grimoire's pages for more answers.

Once you have the listed ingredients, open this book back up for the instructions for the spell. We wish you well!

As fast as the words appeared on the page, they were gone. Without her moving, the book slammed shut and was unable to be opened. When she looked up from the book, the two men in the room were staring at her, waiting for her to say something.

"What did you find," Flynn asked.

"The book gave me the supplies I need for the spell, but the most important one is difficult to figure out," she explained.

"What is it," Flynn looked into her eyes.

"Finding my self-worth," she sighed.

Flynn looked at her in surprise. "You always seemed so sure of yourself; I thought you knew you were worthy," he muttered.

"I am worthy of some things, yes. But I do not feel worthy of love. I mean—look at me," she grabbed handfuls of her straw hair as she said this.

"The hair doesn't make the person," Flynn said soothingly.

"What's in here does," he pointed at her heart.

"Yeah, yeah," she looked at him and rolled her eyes.

"What else is needed, deary," Rumpelstiltskin inquired.

Rapunzel looked in Rumpel's direction with a dark look on her face.

She smiled at him as she said, "One of the things I need is the blood of the caster."

"Done," Rumpelstiltskin said. "Anything to show you that I am on your side."

He bowed his head to show his allegiance.

Rapunzel's head fell to the side. She had not expected this of Rumpelstiltskin, but she was glad he said it all the same.

The other things it said I needed were:

A piece of Moldavite

A flower called Tears of the Moon And Pixie dust.

"That's easy," Flynn and Rumpel said in unison.

"Some of these items may have been difficult to find back in the day, but at least two of these ingredients can be found deep in Sapphire City, in the marketplace by the Sultan's castle," Rumpelstiltskin explained. "The Moldavite will be costly, but to show you my loyalty—I will pay for that. The pixie dust can also be found there. It is coveted in the marketplace and is kept in a well-protected spot, but they should let you in. So long as

they sense no harm to come from you."

"As for the other two ingredients, that might be quite the adventure for you, or at least the flower will be," Flynn said. "Those ingredients reside in lands far from here; it could be a dangerous quest for you to endure alone. But I have the utmost faith in you."

"Me too," said Rumpelstiltskin.

"Thank you for your kindness, both of you," Rapunzel curtsied to the men in the room. "I guess it's time to go track down the easy ingredients first. I'll be headed to the marketplace now."

"Wait—" Rumpel said. "Untie me, please." "Pfft," said Rider.

"I need to give her gold for the moldavite," he explained.

"Fine, but your hands won't be free for long; you better move fast," Flynn said.

"I understand," Rumpel sighed.

He reached into his pocket and produced thirty gold coins.

"This should be enough for both of those items at the marketplace. When you are finished, bring them here.

Then I can tell you where to find the flower. I can't tell you where to find your self-worth, but maybe you will find it along the way," Rumpel told her.

Rapunzel took the gold from his hands and grabbed a jacket. Her nerves were rattled, and she had never been more afraid of failing in her life, but she had to remain positive if this was going to work out right.

"I have something that might be of use to you," Rumpel told her.

When she looked back, he was holding out an old, worn-out piece of paper. Rapunzel took it into her hands and opened it.

A map of the entirety of Sapphire City. She had no idea the city was so large.

"Okay—" she said. "Here goes nothing."

Rapunzel put that jacket on and headed down the stairs. She pushed the blanket to the side and stepped outside, turning back to say goodbye to Flynn. He watched after her as she disappeared into the thicket.

Chapter Sixteen

The Marketplace

R APUNZEL OGLED THE MAP as she stepped into the trees that surrounded the tower. The sun was beaming in her twinkling blue eyes, causing her to squint. She could hear birds chirping around her, and butterflies were blanketing the entire field of flowers. She had never seen anything so beautiful in her life.

She couldn't let this distract her for long; she was determined to find the supplies she needed to break the curse Rumpelstiltskin had cast on her.

Deep in the center of the city is a marketplace: the people passing through were always frantically buying and trading items for money or food. The ambiance of the place was said to feel cloudy, dark, and dense. There was always shouting and people around. All the excitement and fear expanded like the air in a hot air balloon, ready to explode. During their conversations, one in particular, Flynn had told her this was a rundown part of the city. The people here were poor and struggling to survive. The marketplace was filled with the scent of smoke and smog from the factories that surrounded it. He had mentioned a fair share of thieves and charlatans hiding in this area. The thought of going here made her nervous. Although, Flynn had mentioned what was just beyond the marketplace—the palace.

Rapunzel's mind was reeling with what-ifs. Getting lost would be the last thing she needed; she would have to pay close attention to the map Rumpelstiltskin had given her. She pinpointed her place on the map as she stepped into the thicket near the tower. *She found herself grateful that Gothel made her study so hard for all these years.* Looking down at the map, she noticed that in the city's heart was a large palace. She wanted to see it one day.

Rapunzel pried her eyes from the map and looked in front of her. The city on the other side of the tree line was bustling with life. She kept a close eye on each person, watching out for the one person she thought was her mother for her entire life. She followed the map past the store where she had found her family's grimoire just a few nights before.

The map showed that she needed to walk at least two miles west of the shop and turn onto the main street of the city. Rapunzel estimated it would take her at least an hour to reach her destination by foot. She moved as fast as she could whilst taking in the scenery of the city around her.

This was the longest period of time she had ever been alone outside of the tower.

She felt nervous but confident that she would complete her task. Getting her hair back to its normal state was just within her reach; it would just take a little work to get there. She had walked for miles, but it felt like only minutes. When she looked up from the map, she was in an old-fashioned marketplace. Wooden stalls lined the streets, with tapestries hanging over them to block out the sun. The area she walked into was filled with fruits, loaves of bread, vegetables, and other types of foods.

Many of the stall owners looked as if they were barely hanging on, just trying to make their own way. She heard many of them coughing and could hear the children of the stall owners crying and complaining that they were hungry. Every step she took, she took care not to step on or trip over rats. Guards stood at every corner, watching the stalls. They were there to ensure the market ran smoothly and no one stole food or got hurt. The sandstone tiles she walked on in the marketplace brought the whole scene together.

"Here you are," she heard as she saw a woman in deep red garments hand food to small children.

Rapunzel's heart was warmed by the generosity of the people of the world. She found herself even more angry with Gothel for lying to her about the world being such a dangerous place. Rapunzel's eyes widened in fear as she watched the shop owner chastise the woman.

"We don't take kindly to thieves around here," he growled at her. "You'll need to pay for that."

"I—I don't have any money," the woman replied.

Rapunzel wanted to cover her eyes but couldn't as she watched the stall owner grab the woman's arm and raise a sword in the air. A man came to the woman's rescue and said something to the stall owner that made him step back. The clever man snatched a bill out of the stall owner's pocket and handed It to him before he noticed. The two of them rushed off to a spot they needed to climb a ladder to reach. The way he looked at the woman he walked off with was the way Rapunzel dreamed Rider would look at her.

Rapunzel broke her focus from the two of them and peered around the stalls in front of her. All she saw was food; there had to be another area in the marketplace.

The young girl stepped out of her spot and was pushed aside by the guards who ran past.

She followed behind them as they went after the two people, she had watched escape the stall owner. She listened to them fight with the girl who climbed the ladder. She was a woman of importance—someone they should not have been treating with disrespect.

"We have orders to take him to the palace's prison to be executed," she heard the guards say.

The woman said something back to him, but she couldn't make out the words.

"Sorry, we have orders from Jafar," the guard mumbled.

Rapunzel listened to the four of them leave the area before she climbed the ladder. When she reached the top, she was in a small area where someone looked to be sleeping and living—it must have been where the man was staying.

When she looked up from the bedding, her jaw dropped. She was looking out over all of Sapphire City. Deep in the heart of the beautiful buildings was the most spectacular one of them all. The palace. Her breath caught in her throat as she looked out over the palace from the spot where she was standing. She stood there for a few moments before she got her bearings back.

"I need to find the pixie dust," she muttered to herself.

Rapunzel climbed back down the ladder and stopped to take a closer look at the map she was holding in her hands. In one section of the marketplace on the map, she noticed the area

was darkened as if someone was trying to hide it.

She scurried off in that direction. She felt a few shoulders brush past her as she moved. Rapunzel was on high alert— Gothel could be around any corner, ready to pounce. Rapunzel felt as though she had walked in circles for quite some time before she arrived at a secluded section of the marketplace.

"And who—are you, pretty lady," a man asked.

Rapunzel looked at the man in fear. He was short in stature, and he was nearly bald. All the hair on his face was stark white, his eyes were beady, and his back was hunched. He was wearing what appeared to be rags.

"I am looking for a few...magical items," she explained to the small man.

The man smiled at her, showing all three of his teeth.

"Magic—I can help you with. Teeth and hair; I cannot," he chuckled as he rubbed his bald head. "Come on back, I'll show you the goods."

Rapunzel froze in her spot. There was something about this man she was uncomfortable with. Something was not right. "Well," he said, his hand extended toward hers. "You coming?" "Uh—yeah," she responded, stepping into the secluded area. "Tell me, dear, what are you looking for," he asked her.

"I am in search of two very important items," Rapunzel started. "I am looking for a gemstone called Moldavite. Have you heard of it?"

"Moldavite, huh," he said in surprise. "You came at the perfect time; I only have one left."

He led Rapunzel further into the area before motioning for her to stop.

"Stay here; I will go get it for you," he started. "I hope you have the funds for a crystal such as this."

The man crept away and didn't reappear for a few minutes. When he popped back out, he held a large, shining, green stone in his hands. The closer he got to Rapunzel, the more it started to glow. The man's eyes traveled to the stone and back at Rapunzel in surprise.

"I've never seen 'em do that before," he whispered. "It must be meant for you."

As Rapunzel reached for the crystal, it flew out of the man's hand into hers. The power she felt emanating from it was entrancing. She spun it around in her hands, admiring the deep green color. It reminded her of the eyes she had kept seeing on and off.

"How much for the crystal," Rapunzel asked.

"That particular piece is 20 gold coins," the man laughed.

Rapunzel dug in her coat for the coins. When she pulled her hand out, she handed the man twenty gold coins. He looked at her in shock.

"Didn't think you were the type to have money like this," he admitted.

Rapunzel scoffed at him as she dropped the coins into his hands. The audacity of this little old man was astonishing.

"I need one more thing," she interjected. "Pixie dust."

"Pah," the little old man muttered. "Pixie dust."

"What is that supposed to mean," Rapunzel placed her hands on her hips.

"It *means*," the man said. "I figured you would ask for it." "How much for the pixie dust," Rapunzel asked.

The man disappeared again, this time in search of the last item she needed for her spell. He returned quicker this time, with a vial of shiny gold dust in his hands.

"This—" he said, spinning the vial around in his hands. "This comes from a very special fairy. Her magic is highly coveted in many areas. I urge you to proceed with caution. But, if you must have this vial...it will be three gold coins, please."

"Done," Rapunzel said, handing him the coins. "Thank you."

Rapunzel rushed out of the shop, feeling a dire need to get away from the man in the marketplace. As she walked, she strode past the food stalls again. Her stomach was growling from not eating at all that day.

Rapunzel found herself craving a peach.

The straw-haired girl approached the stall and handed the owner two gold coins.

"Ma'am, that's worth ten peaches," he gasped.

"Well, I'll take five, and you can keep the change," Rapunzel smiled at him.

"Th—thank you, kind lady," the young man behind the stall muttered.

Rapunzel felt good performing a good deed for someone in need. She walked away proudly with the peaches in her hand.

Suddenly, she felt each hair on her body stand on end. When she searched the crowd, she noticed Gothel's wiry black hair. Rapunzel ducked into the crowd and hid in the alleyway between two of the buildings behind the stalls. She watched as Gothel walked into the secluded area she had just come from. Gothel spent ample time in the shop. When she emerged from the curtains that led to the shop, she was holding a parcel. Rapunzel strained her eyes to try to see what it was but had no such luck.

Gothel's eyes darted in her direction, but she was able to disappear from view before the witch saw her. Rapunzel waited at least thirty minutes before she stepped out of the alleyway.

She wanted to be sure that Gothel was gone. The young girl feared what the witch might do to her if she got her hands on her.

Rapunzel secured the items in her jacket before walking out of the city's marketplace. As she walked, she daydreamed about the day she would enter the palace in all its glory. She thought about the woman she saw earlier and wondered if she was the daughter of the sultan.

Rapunzel snacked on a peach as she walked. After countless moments of walking, she arrived at the familiar tree line of the thicket that led back to her home. She traveled the beaten path until she stood just outside the tower.

She was proud to have made it past the first hurdle of her journey.

Rapunzel couldn't help but wonder where the flower might be. Her mind started to wander off to the thought of Rumpelstiltskin. Why wasn't his blood the easiest to get? She crept toward the tower, pulling the blanket back to gain access to her home.

Thoughts of Rumpelstiltskin invaded her mind. She still had a niggling feeling that he was not on their side. The thought of it just seemed too good to be true. Besides, men like that are usually out for only one thing—themselves.

Chapter Seventeen

Tears of the Moon

As she pulled back the blanket that gave her access to the tower, she took a deep breath. The first leg of her journey was complete. There were only two more things to do to complete the spell. Finding the elusive flower and taking blood from the monster that ruined her hair. Something had her worried about how hard it would be to get her hands on these items.

Rapunzel ascended the stairs, eager to show Flynn what she had found. When she rounded the corner, she saw Flynn and Rumpelstiltskin asleep. She tiptoed past them and placed the items down on a table in the hall before she woke them up.

Rapunzel cleared her throat, "Must be nice to lounge around while I'm out busting my ass to get everything for this spell."

Rumpelstiltskin was the first one to wake up. His eyes opened sleepily as he looked at Rapunzel in a stupor. He tried to bring his hands up to rub his eyes, but they were bound behind him.

Flynn remained asleep, peacefully snoring away.

A wicked grin crossed Rapunzel's face as she stepped toward her new friend. When she was close enough, she pounced on him. She started to tickle him, and he woke up in a fit of laughter.

"Rapunzel," he said. "you're back."

"Yes, and with two of the items needed for the spell!" she screeched.

"You found them," he said.

"Yes, the place was as run down and scary as you said it was. I saw Gothel, too. I was able to duck out of view before she saw me, though," she shuttered.

Rapunzel turned to Rumpelstiltskin, who remained quiet. She wondered what he was thinking and started to think that he would not be honest about the location of the flower. Now that they were awake, she ventured off to the table in the hall to grab the items.

"That is the largest piece of Moldavite that I have seen in years," Rumpel informed her. "I can't get past the glowing, though. They usually don't do that. Although, with you being a descendant of the Ashenbrook bloodline—I could see things being more intense around you."

Rapunzel suddenly looked fearful. She remembered the strange man she had met at the marketplace. There was something off about him, and she had to know what.

"What is wrong, Rapunzel," Flynn sat up as he said this.

"There was this little old man—" she trailed off.

"And?" Rumpelstiltskin said impatiently.

"He was a small man with a hunched back. He was bald with three teeth. Something about him creeped me out—" Rapunzel fell silent.

"Jafar—" Rider said.

"Jafar?" she asked. "I heard the guards talking about him; from the way they were talking, it seemed he was at the palace."

"He can change forms; it's just another tool in his magical arsenal," Flynn explained. "He owns half that city, and he watches the people under that guise and pretends to be one of them."

"Watches them?" Rapunzel asked.

"For fuel to use against them when he gets angry. He is a very cruel man, not someone you want to jump into bed with," Rider said.

"He's right, deary. Steer clear," Rumpel growled.

"Oh, I saw Gothel visit him, too," Rapunzel piped up. "She spent a lot of time in that secluded area and reappeared with a parcel—I don't know what it was, though." "That evil scheming—" Rumpel started.

Rapunzel looked at him in shock. Some of her doubts about him started to fade.

"Do you know what it was," Rapunzel asked.

"I have an idea, but that is not what we need to focus on right now. Did you want to know the whereabouts of that flower or not," he asked.

"I'm listening," Rapunzel responded.

"I hear the witch is staying at her old place, deeper in the woods. You will have to head over there when you know she is gone. In her garden, there is a hidden place, and you will see a glowing white flower that shines in the moonlight," he explained. "When the moon's light hits it just right, it looks as if there are water droplets on its petals, hence the name—tears of the moon."

"When is the witch usually away from that place," Rider asked, lifting himself from his spot.

"We will need a distraction—" Rumpel told them. "I can be your bait, pretend to be interested in her again, and lure her to the hotel for the night."

"Absolutely not," Flynn started. "How are we to know you won't double-cross us?"

"You'll just have to trust me," Rumpelstiltskin winked at them. He raised his two first fingers together in the air. "Scout's honor."

Rapunzel looked over at Flynn. Both of them were nervous about the trust they were about to put into the man who caused this whole catastrophe.

"It might be the only way," Rapunzel said softly.

Flynn stepped toward Rumpelstiltskin and reached down to untie his hands.

"I'll have to leave so he can use his magic again," he said. "You sure about this Rapunzel?"

Rapunzel nodded. "As sure as I'll ever be. It is what needs to be done.

As his hands were freed from the sheets that bound his hands, he reached up to rub the sleep from his eyes.

"Much better," he said. "You better be on your way now,

Flynnie."

Flynn descended the stairs and left the tower. Rapunzel heard a loud cracking noise as Rumpelstiltskin vanished into thin air.

A Few Hours Later

Rumpelstiltskin brushed himself off as he entered the pub in Sapphire City. He sat at the bar and waved down the bartender.

"Whiskey on the rocks, my good man," he called to him.

Seconds later, a glass slid in his direction. Rumpel grabbed the glass and took a few swigs of the liquor he ordered. The burning of the alcohol sliding down his throat was cathartic after the day he had had. When he placed the glass back down on the bar, he rubbed his wrists. They were still sore from being bound with the sheet all day.

As he rubbed his wrists, he felt a pair of eyes bore into his back. When he turned around, Gothel was sitting at a table across the room. The look on her face was one of pure hatred. He grabbed his glass from the bar and stood from his stool.

"Fancy seeing you here, deary," Rumpel called out to Gothel.

Gothel turned her nose up and looked the other way, trying to ignore the fact that the man in front of her existed—the man who shattered her heart and reminded her why she hated love in the first place.

"That's no way to greet an old flame," Rumpel growled.

He walked over to her and touched her shoulder, watching a chill take over her entire body. His touch—always did something to her that she couldn't explain. He used this to his advantage. Rumpelstiltskin traced his fingers down her back, watching her melt in his hands.

"Did you miss me," he whispered in her ear.

She groaned, unable to speak. The way her body responded to his touch was second nature. It wasn't something so easily controllable. As much as she tried to hate it, every fiber of her being wanted more.

Gothel grabbed Rumpel's hand. "What are you insinuating, sir," she asked.

She jumped when his hand grazed her bits.

"I'm insinuating that you ride me harder than you ever have before," he whispered in her ear.

Suddenly, her sex was dripping with desire.

"I was hoping you would say that," she admitted, kissing him on the cheek.

Rumpelstiltskin took her face in his hands, devouring her lips with his. He bit her lip, causing her to cry out as his dick grew harder and harder in his pants.

"Are you ready to go? Same hotel, same room. Sound good," he asked.

"Fantastic," she breathed. "When do we leave?"

Back at the Tower

"I know you have to go this alone, but I really wish I could come with you this time," Rider told Rapunzel. He grabbed her hand and patted it.

"I wish you could, too," she said, staring into his eyes.

The sun had set a few hours ago. This left behind the radiant beams of the moon, lighting up the blackened sky.

"I have to go—" Rapunzel trailed off.

Rider stared at the ground, wondering if kissing her would be the worst distraction.

"Before you go," he said quietly.

"Hmm," she spun around, and Flynn was standing so close she could feel his breath.

Flynn took her face in his hands and planted a gentle kiss on her lips.

"For good luck," he said.

"Thanks, I'll need it," Rapunzel said as she backed away. She wasn't sure about how to respond, but she did know that she had fallen for Flynn Rider—something she didn't intend to do.

If she didn't feel worthy of anything earlier, she did now. But she knew Flynn would never feel the same way about her that she did about him.

Unrequited love—a searing lash upon a wary heart.

As Rapunzel rushed out of the tower, she didn't notice Flynn following close behind her. He stopped at the blanket and watched her wander off into the forest around her. He wished more than anything that he had time to explain the kiss, but she moved too fast.

She didn't know where to find the witch's cottage, but she knew it wasn't going to be directly in Sapphire City. She remembered Gothel telling her stories of a small farmhouse with a luscious garden, but she hadn't known it was real until now.

Something in Rapunzel told her to travel further west. Following her intuition, she stepped out of a thick patch of trees into a field. On one end of the field stood a lonely, rundown house. On the other was a beautiful farmhouse—with the most bountiful garden Rapunzel had ever seen.

Something about the run-down house drew her in. She needed to see what was in there before she could carry out the rest of the plan. Rapunzel crept across the pasture and approached the house. As she stepped in front of the door, the door swung open.

The smell of dust and rot filled her senses. Her nose scrunched as she stepped into the house. When she looked to her left, there was a small kitchen. Laying on the floor was a gun and a skeleton whose skull had a hole in it from a gunshot.

The sight of this made Rapunzel's stomach churn. She forced the contents of her stomach back down her throat as she moved forward. When she moved into the living room, she saw the walls overflowing with portraits of a loving couple. Rapunzel's eyes caught a set of familiar green eyes. When she stepped closer to the picture, she knew in her gut that this woman was her mother.

Rapunzel took the picture from the wall and backed out of the house. As she backed away, she noticed a shallow grave.

Rest In Peace

Beloved Wife & Mother – EVE

Tears filled the young woman's eyes as she realized the body in the house was her father's. Both parents were deceased, probably by the fault of the monster of a woman who raised her. Rapunzel held the picture close to her chest as she crept toward the cottage.

Before she traveled to the garden, she had to see how Gothel lived. Rapunzel approached the door to the cottage and had to break it open to get in. Once the door swung open, Rapunzel saw a pile of blankets on the floor. The house was empty aside from them. She realized just how much Gothel had given up when she left Rapunzel behind.

She wandered around the dark house for a few minutes, trying to gain any insight into Gothel that she could. Over her short time in the house, she felt the hatred that had grown inside of Gothel toward her. She never understood why their relationship ended up that way. Rapunzel always tried to be the best daughter she could be.

Rapunzel backed out of the house, feelings of dread swallowing her whole. She made her way over to the greenery of the garden. It was dark, but the full moon illuminated the beauty of the fruit trees and vegetables. The garden was a labyrinth that Rapunzel found herself struggling to navigate. She was stunned at the genius work behind the well-placed fruit trees, grains, and vegetables.

Rapunzel roamed the labyrinth for quite some time before she noticed something glowing in the center. On a small table in the center of the garden was a flower kept in a glass container. The flower was as white as the light of the moon, and the droplets could be seen on the petals from the direction of the moon's light.

"Tears of the Moon," Rapunzel breathed as she reached for the container.

Once the container was safely in her arms with the picture of her parents, Rapunzel found her way out of the maze and headed back toward the tower she called home.

Chapter Eighteen

Everything She's Worth

It was close to midnight by the time Rapunzel made it back to the tower. The night air created a rosy pink look on her cheeks, and her hair picked up grass and sticks on her way back. Rapunzel's whirring emotions had worn her down for the night, and she was ready to climb into bed and drift off into a peaceful slumber.

As her feet hit the stairs to the tower, she couldn't shake the feeling that something odd was going on. She sensed no danger, but something—felt off. Rapunzel peered around the corner of the stairs to see candles lit all throughout the main room of the tower. Upon further inspection, rose petals were spread across the floor and furniture. Rapunzel had never seen anything more romantic.

When she walked into the main room, her senses were filled with the scent of steak and mashed potatoes. When she looked to the right, Rider stood in the kitchen, cooking a hearty meal. "What's all this," Rapunzel asked as she walked toward Flynn. Flynn spun around; his cheeks flushed with a bashful glow. He looked lost for words, but his mouth still managed to articulate what he had meant to tell her before she left.

"This—" he started. "This is all for you."

"For me," she repeated. "But why?"

Flynn approached her, grabbing her hips with his hand. Her breath caught in her throat as he pressed his lips into hers once again. This time, his tongue forced her mouth open, and he kissed her feverishly. The heat in the room skyrocketed as their hands explored each other's bodies.

Flynn pulled away as things were getting intense.

"But first, dinner," he explained. He swooped past the table and pulled out a chair, motioning for Rapunzel to sit.

Rapunzel gracefully sat in her seat as she watched Flynn carry plates of food out of the kitchen. The food he had prepared smelled heavenly, and Rapunzel could not wait to dive in. Flynn set the plates on the table, and before he sat, he lit the red candle that he had placed in the center of the table.

When Flynn sat down, the ambiance of the entire room shifted. The light and airy feeling of friendship had somehow reshaped itself into something deeper. Rapunzel had no idea

when this change took place in Flynn, but the look in his eyes— stirred a flame in her that would never burn out.

Flynn poured each of them a glass of chardonnay and raised his in the air.

"To us," he said. "And to happily ever after!"

"Us," Rapunzel gasped. "To us," she said with more gusto.

She placed her cup on the table and grabbed a fork and a knife, taking care to remember to eat more like a lady this time. She could feel Flynn watching her, his eyes never losing sight of the beauty that sat before him.

The two of them supped in peace, their bodies aching for the tender moments they would share after dinner and a drink.

"How was it at the witch's place," he asked.

Rapunzel stirred in her seat.

"I discovered far more than her cottage," she admitted. "I know what my parents looked like, and I know they are both

dead. Probably because of Gothel."

Flynn reached across the table and wiped a tear from her cheek, caressing her face afterward.

"I—I'm so sorry," he said, his expression shifting from lustful to sad.

"It's okay—at least I know they loved me," she replied, nuzzling her face into his hand.

He grabbed her hand. "You found the flower," he asked. "Yes, her garden was quite a maze. But I made it through," Rapunzel smiled shyly.

As they finished dinner, Flynn placed the dishes in the sink and blew the candle out. He walked over to Rapunzel and wrapped his arms around her, bringing his lips to her forehead.

"You are worthy," he said.

"But I thought I wasn't your type," Rapunzel sighed.

"I was wrong; you are my dream come true," Rider said as he blushed.

Rapunzel looked up into his eyes as he stared down at her. She could feel his erection pressing into her. *This certainly wasn't the night she expected.*

Flynn brought his lips to her neck, gently kissing and sucking. He took the sleeve of her dress and slid it downward, revealing her shoulder. When her shoulder was exposed, he gave it a gentle kiss.

"Are you sure this is what you want," he asked her.

"This is what I have wanted since the first time I laid eyes on you," she admitted.

Flynn chuckled as he picked a stick out of her straw hair.

"Even with hair full of sticks and grass, you are still the most beautiful woman I have ever seen," he whispered in her ear.

Rapunzel took his hand and led him to her bedroom, where she slid her dress off. When her bra hit the ground, her nipple stood erect for him.

Rider took his time soaking in every inch and detail of her body. He tore his shirt off and let his pants and boxers hit the ground. Once his clothes were off, he pushed Rapunzel onto the bed.

"I am into very dark things, but I want our first time to be remembered as something special," he explained.

Rapunzel nodded as she watched him move toward her.

"Every moment we have spent together has been special," she said as he climbed on the bed.

He shimmied his way upward, allowing their skin to touch in every way possible. When he made it to her face, he kissed her so deeply that her breath was stolen.

He continued by trailing soft kisses down her neck to her collarbone. Rapunzel arched her back as his mouth found her breasts. He took care to pay special attention to each nipple as he sucked on them and flicked them with his tongue.

Rapunzel's waist moved upward as Flynn's hand traveled toward her bits. Low moans could be heard coming from each of them as the mood of the room escalated.

"Mm," Flynn heard as he inserted two fingers inside of her.

His thumb found her clit and circled it with expertise. His arched fingers inside of her had an orgasm building within minutes. He grinned as her pussy locked around his fingers, and warm fluid came rushing out. The sounds of Rapunzel's ecstasy were music to his ears.

"You just wait, baby," he growled as he brought his fingers to her lips. "I'm not done with you yet."

He inserted his fingers into her mouth, letting her taste the sweet fluid that she left on his fingers.

"Taste yourself," he said. "This is the sweetest I have ever had."

Rapunzel took his fingers into her mouth and licked up every last drop of her juices.

"Oh—" she exclaimed. "I do taste sweet."

With those words, Flynn kissed her lips, lightly tugging at them with his teeth.

"My turn," Rapunzel said, smiling darkly.

Flynn moaned as he felt Rapunzel's hand slide down his body. "Stand up," Rapunzel commanded.

Flynn rose to his feet, his breathing quickening in excitement.

"Come here, big boy," she said, wrapping her hand around his cock.

Rapunzel stroked his cock as she took the tip of him into her mouth. Flynn could feel her tongue swirling around it as her lips carefully tucked away her teeth. She stayed here for a moment, building anticipation before she took his entire length into her throat. Rider pumped himself into her mouth repeatedly, yelling out as his warm fluid dripped down the back of her throat.

"You—are a goddess," he told Rapunzel.

"You're not so bad yourself, sir," she chuckled.

Rapunzel rose to meet his face and kissed him, exploring each part of his mouth with her tongue. Rider laid her back as he climbed on top of her. The two lay there for a few moments, enjoying the skin-to-skin contact, before Rider spoke up.

"Get on your hands and knees," he whispered in her ear.

Rapunzel felt chills ride up and down her back, as she obeyed his wishes. Rider slid his fingers down her back, tracing patterns all the way down. Her body shivered with delight as he brought his rock-hard dick to her entrance and teased her with it. Her entrance throbbed as she waited for him to fuck her. Right as she thought he was going to slam into her, he pulled away. Rapunzel then felt a finger slide into her asshole. As she was lost in the sensation of fullness, he buried his dick so far inside of her that she yelled out.

Flynn took it slow at first, relishing the tightness that was her pussy. He could feel her warming up as he pumped; she pushed back into him, her body begging for more.

"Harder," Rapunzel cried.

Flynn had never heard sexier words. He pulled himself nearly out of her and slammed back in with full force. He pounded into her over and over as he pumped his finger in and out of her asshole. After a half hour of continuous thrusting and pumping, Rapunzel's body melted, her pussy locking around his cock as she cried in ecstasy.

He pulled out of her, and they lay together side by side. Flynn looked Rapunzel in the eyes with a look of pure love and adoration. He reached his hand up and caressed her face, sliding a piece of straw hair behind her ear.

"I love you—" he started.

Rapunzel froze. These are words she never thought she would hear coming from the likes of Flynn Rider. She leaned in and planted a soft kiss on his lips before responding. "I love you more."

"I hope you have always known that you are worthy of every good thing this universe has to offer you—" he trailed off as he got lost in her deep blue eyes.

"I—I," she said. "Thank you."

A wave of pride and relief washed over her as she found herself believing his words.

"I never felt worthy of anything," she admitted. "Especially not—like this," she lifted her straw hair, entangled with sticks and grass.

Flynn leaned in and kissed her.

"I'd go to the ends of the earth for you," he touched his nose to hers.

Something in the room changed as he said this. It was as if a weight had been lifted off both of their shoulders. Flynn noticed a supernatural glow take over the woman in front of him.

"I think—" he said with a smile. "I think now you know your true worth, and I have never been prouder."

Silence washed over Rapunzel like a wave. These are words she had never heard in her short life.

"No one has ever been proud of me before," she said as a shy grin crossed her face.

She watched as Rider melted next to her, then leaned in for a tender kiss.

"I've never had anyone to be proud of before—" he started. "I've always been the loner type—trust really isn't my thing," he admitted. "Never had so much as a single friend, only people

I've used to get what I need." "Are you saying—" Rapunzel started.

"You're the only person I trust and the only one I ever have trusted." He said. "I lay my heart bare to you; please be kind to it."

"I will guard it with my life," Rapunzel sighed. "I would kill for you—just to know you're safe."

Rider leaned in and kissed her, holding her closer than he ever had.

"My heart is yours, Rapunzel," he breathed. "If you'll have it." "Mine has been yours since we first met," she giggled.

"And I will keep it with me—forever," he said as he tapped his finger to her nose.

Rapunzel fell asleep in Rider's arms, and it wasn't long before Rider drifted off to sleep, too.

Chapter Nineteen

The Blood of an Impish Man

Rider's eyes snapped open as he heard a loud cracking noise in front of them. When his eyes were able to focus, he noticed it was none other than Rumpelstiltskin standing in front of them. Rapunzel felt Rider stirring and started to wake as Rumpelstiltskin approached the bed.

"I told ya, you can trust me," he said with a sheepish grin.

"Did you get the flower?"

Rapunzel yawned and stretched before she could form any words. "Damn, skippy, I did," she said, holding both thumbs in the air.

Flynn chuckled at the playfulness he witnessed coming from Rapunzel.

"I knew you could do it," Rumpel said, holding both of his thumbs in the air. "We need to be quick; it won't be long before she realizes something is amiss at her cottage."

Flynn and Rapunzel jumped out of bed, forgetting neither of them were dressed. Rumpel's eyes wandered over to the delicious curves on Rapunzel's body as the sheets hit the ground. She immediately covered up when she realized she didn't have any clothes on.

"I'll—uh, see myself out while you get dressed," Rumple stuttered as he backed out of the room.

Once he was out of the room, Rider and Rapunzel fell into a fit of giggles. Rapunzel grabbed her clothes and got dressed as Rider dressed himself. When they exited the room, they noticed a solemn look on Rumpelstiltskin's face.

"What's wrong, Rumpel," Rapunzel asked.

"I know you thought this part would be the easiest...you know—getting my blood," Rumpel muttered. "Not to burst your bubble, but I am invulnerable to most man-made weapons."

"What do you mean," Rider asked.

Rapunzel's face fell, but she knew she had to stay strong if she was going to complete her quest.

"There is one item, though, that will cut through me like butter," Rumpel informed them. "However, it might be difficult to locate."

"Why is that?" Rapunzel asked.

"It was hidden away by my wife a long time ago. When we first were married. Before she wanted to cut my head off," he explained.

"What is this so-called item," Rapunzel inquired.

"It's a dagger if you must know—" Rumpel answered her. "A dagger that was cursed by the witch I stole my magic from." "That narrows it down—" Rider rolled his eyes.

"This dagger is pure black, with black snakeskin for a hilt," he explained. "You can feel it when you are near it; it has a very dark and peculiar energy."

"Where is this—dagger," Rapunzel asked.

"No idea," Rumpelstiltskin answered, shrugging his shoulders.

His eyes wandered toward the direction of the grimoire.

"What do you mean? You don't know," Flynn screamed. "What part of "hidden away"—don't you understand?" Rumpelstiltskin scolded.

"There has to be a way to find it," Rapunzel whined.

"I have a feeling Rapunzel's ancestors would know the answer to this. The Ashenbrook witches kept a close eye on that witch and her magic," he said, rubbing his hands together.

Rumpel walked toward the large bean bag chair and plopped down, making himself at home. He watched as Rapunzel darted toward the grimoire, desperate to find the answers she was seeking.

Rapunzel picked up the grimoire and thumbed through it as the words on the pages began to appear right in front of her.

"Blade of the Depraved," she read.

This blade was created for the sole purpose of taking the life of an immortal. When it comes to this blade, there is no simple cut for blood; there is only death.

Rapunzel shuddered as she read this. Rumpelstiltskin's face twisted in curiosity.

"What's in the book, deary?" he asked.

"I'm still reading," she answered. "Give me just a moment."

The Blade of the Depraved was procured centuries ago by a young woman looking to protect her husband. No one knows its exact hiding place. However, there is a way to find it.

Rapunzel's brow furrowed as she read further. Both men in the room were riddled with curiosity; Rapunzel had yet to speak a word.

"Scrying for Magical Items," Rapunzel read aloud.

"That sounds like something that would really help you," Rumpelstiltskin said.

"What is scrying," Rider and Rapunzel asked at the same time.

"It is a way for magical folk to find lost items," Rumpel informed them.

"It says I need a piece of your hair," Rapunzel told him.

Rumpel reached up and plucked a few hairs from his head.

"Done," he said. "What's next?"

"Uh—a map and a crystal on a rope," she said, confused.

"I got you, my sweet," Rumpelstiltskin reached into his pocket and produced a crystal on a metal chain.

"And a map," Rapunzel asked.

"That would be in your pocket," Rumpelstiltskin told her.

"The map of Sapphire City," Rapunzel asked.

"Precisely, deary," he replied.

Attach the personal effect to the crystal and hold it over the map. The pendulum will swing, but after a few seconds, it will zone in on the location of the item you are looking for. Let it fall, do not keep it in the air.

Rapunzel wrapped the strands of hair around the pendulum as Rider spread the map out on the table. The crystal swung wildly around the map and fell onto the location of the dagger.

"The palace—" Rapunzel's voice broke off.

"You are amazing, Rapunzel, but I worry about you entering that palace alone," Flynn said, concerned for her well-being.

"I know—but if I am going to get back to the way I used to be, I *have* to do this," she whined.

"I understand," Rider said. "But take this with you, for good luck."

Rider reached his hands around his neck and undid the clasp for the dog tag necklace he was wearing. When he had it removed, he placed it into Rapunzel's hand.

"These were my father's," he said. "He was a war veteran and the bravest man I ever knew. Please take this with you to keep you safe and give you the boost of luck you need."

Rapunzel's eyes teared up as she took the dog tags from Rider.

"Th-Thank you," she stumbled on her words.

"Anything for my princess," Rider said as he kissed her lips.

"I guess I should be on my way," she told him.

"We will be right here waiting for you when you return," Rumpelstiltskin said.

"Wait," Rapunzel said, placing her hand on Rider's shoulder.

"I need to speak with you. In private."

The two of them descended the stairs of the tower and stepped outside.

"The grimoire told me the dagger will kill Rumpelstiltskin," she breathed. "Should we go along with this?"

"It's okay," Rumpelstiltskin said, walking down the stairs behind them. "I've lived a long life, and I have lost much. It would be nice to see my daughter again."

The Palace

Rapunzel tip-toed around the back of the palace, knowing the catacombs were the only way into the palace unnoticed. As she descended the stone steps, the rats under her feet made her shriek.

"Rats," she said under her breath. "I hate rats."

She stepped through the threshold of the catacombs, taking in the elaborate stone pillars that lined the entire place. Her hair dragged behind her, picking up dust and dirt as she walked. When she made it to the end of the hall, the only way to go was right. As she rounded the corner, she stepped back behind the wall.

Near the stairs exiting the catacombs was a tall man. He wore black robes and a tall black and gold hat. A curly mustache flowed across the area under his nose, and he had a small tuft of hair below his lower lip. The man's eyes were dark and sinister. Being stopped, she turned toward the area next to her. She had to stifle a gasp after seeing piles of bones sitting in a nook in the room.

"How's the street rat," the man said to someone Rapunzel couldn't see.

"Miserable," he said.

As Rapunzel peeked around the corner, she saw the man's lips curl into a smile.

"Good, keep it that way," he said.

"What do you want me to do with the monkey," the guard asked.

"That's a worry for another day, I've got shit to do," he growled as he shuffled past the guard in front of him.

Rapunzel could hear the heel of his shoe clacking on the stone floor. Not long after he was out of view, the guard ascended the stairs, leaving the catacombs. She waited a few moments before stepping out of her place.

The young woman tip-toed up the stairs, grabbing the edge of the door before looking into the palace before her.

The white and gold marble floors took her breath away. The ornate pillars took the shape of elephants and flowers. The double doors to the palace were open, and the fresh air filled the room, leaving a scent of freshly made bread and fruit from the marketplace.

As the last person left the main room, Rapunzel scurried through. She entered a hallway on the other side. Hearing a voice near her, she pushed a large oak door open to remain unseen. She turned around, looking at the room that surrounded her. The room was full of ancient relics and odd-looking items.

Stepping further into the room, she noticed an ornate silver box. She could feel her ancestors whispering to her to look inside. As she stepped closer to it, the box began to glow. Rapunzel reached for the box, wrapping her hands around it. Rapunzel took a deep breath as she lifted the cover to the box. When the cover fell to the side, she saw a deep black blade, as Rumpelstiltskin described.

She ran her fingers over the snakeskin hilt, her fingertips taking in the scaly texture. Rapunzel wrapped her fingers around the hilt, removing the blade from the box. She carefully tucked it away in her hair, where she knew it would be safe. Placing the box back in its exact spot, she backed away to leave the room.

As the double doors creaked open, she found herself face to face with the intimidating man she had seen in the catacombs.

"And who might you be little miss," the words escaped from his lips.

He grabbed her by the arm, tugging her out of the room.

Rapunzel froze, unable to answer.

"You'll be going to the dungeon—now," he said as he continued dragging her across the palace.

"No, please!" Rapunzel screamed, trying to break away.

"Oh, yes," he responded.

"Jafar," a woman's voice screamed from across the room. "Let her go!"

"I don't bow down to the likes of women," he spat on the ground.

He pulled harder on Rapunzel's arm, forcing her down a different set of stairs than she had used when she entered the palace. The dungeon reeked of sweat, piss, and soil. Before she could blink, Jafar threw her into a cell and slammed the door.

"I'll see to it that you never get out," Jafar said as he scoffed and walked away.

Rapunzel brought her hands to her face and sobbed. She was at a loss for how she was going to make it out of the palace and back home. Her mind wandered to Flynn, and her heart shattered even more.

She was pulled out of her self-pity session when she heard a man clear his voice from the cell next to her. He was chained to the wall; she didn't have it as bad as him. When she calmed herself down enough, she remembered the dagger she had hidden in her hair.

She began to dig through her straw hair until she felt the edge of the dark blade she had stolen earlier. Rapunzel removed it from her hair and walked toward the door, looking in each direction to be sure a guard wasn't watching.

There was a guard sleeping in a chair a few feet away; she would have to be quiet. Rapunzel dug at the lock with the dagger, nearly dropping it when it started to change in form. The once sharp dagger was now a black, ornate key. She wriggled it and twisted it in the cell's lock, and the door swung open. Rapunzel caught it just before it clattered against the other cell's bars.

She snuck past the snoring guard, taking care to make as little noise as possible, and made her way out of the castle.

Chapter Twenty

Seething Vengeance

Rapunzel ducked under the blanket leading into the tower. As she ascended the stairs, she ran into Flynn, who took her into his arms and kissed her like she had been gone for years. A tear rolled down her cheek as they kissed. He grabbed her hands, noticing the bruises on her wrists.

"What happened?" Rider asked with unease.

"I met Jafar," Rapunzel shuddered. "He caught me in the palace and grabbed me by the wrists and threw me in a cell. If you couldn't tell, he was not gentle with me."

Rider took her in his arms, kissing her on the forehead.

"I'll kill him if I ever see him," he growled. "But for right now, you're here, and you're safe. That is all that matters. We will get the dagger, somehow."

"I have the dagger," Rapunzel whispered to him.

"You got it," Flynn said, his jaw dropping open.

Rapunzel lifted two thumbs in the air. "Damn straight, I did." The two of them ascended the stairs into the main room of the tower. When they turned the corner, they noticed Rumpelstiltskin with his head buried in his hands.

"What's wrong," Rapunzel asked in a softening tone.

"I feel like my blood is boiling, and my skin is tearing to shreds," he cried, squeezing his eyes shut in pain. "You got the dagger—didn't you?"

"I did," Rapunzel wept. "I'm so sorry it has to be this way."

"It's okay," Rumpel sighed. "Go get the grimoire; I'm sure your ancestors are eager to give you directions on how to restore your hair."

Rapunzel ran off to her room, wrapping her hands around the grimoire. She walked into the main room; her face white with dread. As she held the book out, the pages of the book turned until they fell open on a particular page.

A bright golden light shimmered from the grimoire's pages.

"Now that you have all the pieces to this spell, we can reveal the inner workings of the magic and guide you to success. You will need a large bowl. Place the moldavite in the bowl and drop as much blood from the imp as you can. Repeat this mantra three times: "Ad vitam capillus paleas,"

As you repeat this mantra, sprinkle the pixie dust in your hair, then place the dagger in the bowl. Know your worth, as you have recently found, and the spell will be complete.

Rapunzel's pulse pounded beneath her skin, making it hard to gain her composure. When she found the strength to collect herself, she shuffled to the kitchen to find a large bowl. Her heart clogged with guilt as she wandered through the main room, gathering the rest of the supplies.

Rapunzel placed the items in the center of the room and skulked over to Rumpelstiltskin. When he stood up, she opened her arms wide for a hug. Rumpelstiltskin wrapped his arms around her and hugged her tight.

"See you in another life, deary," he sniffled.

Rapunzel placed moldavite in the bowl, her arms quivering in unease. After she placed it in the center of the bowl, Rumpel joined her in the center of the room, holding out his arm. Rapunzel grabbed the dagger, holding it to her new friend's arm.

"Do it," he said. "Please don't worry about me, live your life, get revenge, live happily ever after."

Rapunzel pierced his arm with the dagger, and blood poured over the moldavite crystal. As she did this, her ears were filled with screams of torment. As the blood finished pouring over the moldavite, Rumpel's voice caught in his throat, eyes rolling into the back of his head. Not long after, his strength gave way, and he fell to the floor.

Rapunzel repeated the mantra as she sprinkled pixie dust into her hair. Trying to remember her worth, she placed the dagger in the bowl with tears streaming down her cheeks. As she finished the spell, shimmering golden light rose from the bowl and surrounded her, lifting her in the air. As she twirled around, the straw in her hair broke into pieces, revealing the deep raven-black hair that she had before.

When the magic released her, Rider stepped in front of her with eyes full of warmth. He pulled her in for a kiss, running his fingers through her hair.

"I—I'm me again," Rapunzel crooned.

"You have always been you," Rider said.

Rapunzel rolled her eyes at his corny response.

"Marry me," Flynn proposed as he dropped to one knee.

Rapunzel burst into tears and nodded slowly, her hands covering her mouth.

"Yes, Yes, a million times yes," Rapunzel shrieked in excitement.

Rider scooped his fiancé up, carrying her to her bed. When he placed her on the bed, Rapunzel held a finger up and opened her mouth to speak.

"Wait," she giggled. "I have a surprise. Lay here and wait for me, I will be right back."

Rapunzel rushed off to the room that was once Gothel's. Under the bed, she took the toys she had used with Ferdinand, excited for Rider to use them on her. When she returned to the bedroom, she waved them in the air.

Rider's lips curled into a dark smile. "How did you know what I was into?"

"Me too," she said, tossing the tools to him. "Show me a good time."

"With pleasure," he growled as he pulled her into bed with him.

He ripped her clothes off, undressing himself afterward. Rapunzel's eyes traveled to his rock-hard erection, and she squirmed in need.

"Are you sure this is what you want," he implored.

"More than I have ever wanted anything in my life besides marrying you, of course," she giggled.

Flynn grabbed the flogger from the bed, waggling his eyebrows suggestively. He raised the flogger into the air, striking it downward into Rapunzel's abdomen. He struck her a few times before putting his hand on her pinkened skin.

"So irresistible," he said.

Flynn dropped his face to her thighs, trailing soft kisses upward toward her bits. When he reached her sex, he inserted two fingers into her entrance and licked and flicked her clit as she screamed out in euphoria. He brought his other hand to her ass, pumping his forefinger into her asshole repeatedly. The sound of Rapunzel moaning was music to his ears. It wasn't long before her pussy clamped around his fingers, and juices splashed all over his face, waiting to be licked clean.

Rider kissed his way up her body, inserting the two fingers he used to pleasurable her into her mouth. Sounds of approval could be heard coming from her throat. He pinched and played with her nipples, causing them to harden in response, then reached back on the bed and produced a brand-new pair of nipple clamps that he used to create more pleasure for her. Once he clamped them to her nipples, her back arched in response.

Flynn kissed her neck, sucking on it and making his way to her face. His tongue found its way into her mouth, never wanting to leave. He kissed her more deeply than he ever had. Rapunzel felt him raise her legs in the air over his shoulders. He thrust himself balls deep inside of her and pulled out slowly, only to slam back into her again.

Together, they spiraled in ecstasy, basking in the afterglow of lovemaking. As he pulled up, he brought his dick to her face.

"Taste yourself, "he said.

Rapunzel took the length of him into her mouth, licking it clean and massaging him with her tongue until she felt warm ropes of cum slide down the back of her throat.

Rider lay beside her, pulling her into his embrace and then gently kissing her forehead.

"I love you," he said.

"I love you too," Rapunzel said, nuzzling his chest.

They fell asleep in each other's arms until morning when they heard a blood-curdling scream come from the main room. The two of them jumped to their feet, getting dressed as quickly as possible.

As Rapunzel approached the room, she saw Gothel on her knees sobbing. She looked years older, and her skin was alabaster white.

"My love," she cried. "What has happened to you." She looked up from his body to see Rapunzel and Rider.

"You—" she sobbed. "YOU DID THIS!"

Gothel raised her finger in the air and shouted a curse.

"MORTUUS EST MIHI," she screamed, as a black beam of light streamed from her fingers.

"No," Rider yelled as he jumped in front of the bolt.

As the bolt of magic hit him, he screamed as his skin charred.

After moments of agony he fell to the floor, deceased.

Rapunzel fell to the floor, sobbing at his side.

"We were supposed to grow old together," she caressed his face as she kissed him goodbye.

"How could you?" she screamed at Gothel. "You selfish evil bitch."

"Me, Evil?" Gothel scoffed. "You killed the love of MY life first."

"Hardly a love at all," Rapunzel screamed. "He went to bed with you to distract you, and helped me to lift the curse that you forced him to cast!"

Gothel remained silent.

"He called you a monster and gave his life willingly to get away from you," Rapunzel barked.

She could see tears streaming down Gothel's face. Rapunzel hated that she cared for her. As she was distracted, Gothel lifted the bloody dagger from the bowl and lunged at Rapunzel.

Before she could get close to Rapunzel, the raven-black hair that topped her head wildly raised into the air, wrapping around Gothel.

"Let—me—-go," Gothel squirmed, trying to break free.

"No—this ends, now!" Rapunzel screamed.

Rapunzel's hair wrapped tighter around the woman who raised her. Her eyes began to bulge out of her head.

"Please, I love you," Gothel choked.

"NO, YOU DON'T," Rapunzel screamed.

Gothel began to change. Her skin wrinkled, her eyes drooping, her hair turning white. Rapunzel watched as Gothel aged rapidly and turned to dust, falling to the ground. A breeze swept through the room, carrying Gothel away until she was no more.

Rapunzel fell to the ground, screaming in despair. Just when she thought she had lost everything — her hair turned golden once again. Her beautiful locks wrapped around her lovers body, removing the scorch marks and charred skin.

It was then that she saw it — his eyes opened. He was alive! Rapunzel ran for her lover and wrapped her arms around him, and kissed him like she'd never let him go again.

And they lived happily ever after.

The End

Also by L. R. Crow

Desolation of the Sea

Sins of Snow

Milton Keynes UK
Ingram Content Group UK Ltd.
UKHW022124291124
451915UK00010B/515